❧ The Newbery Medal ❧

The Newbery Medal, the first award of its kind, is the official recognition by the American Library Association of the most distinguished children's book published during the previous year. It is the primary and best known award in the field of children's literature.

Frederic G. Melcher first proposed the award, to be named after the eighteenth-century English bookseller John Newbery, to the Children's Librarian Section of the American Library Association meeting on June 21, 1921. His proposal was met with enthusiastic acceptance and was officially adopted by the ALA Executive Board in 1922. The award itself was commissioned by Mr. Melcher to be created by the artist Rene Paul Chambellan.

Melcher's formal agreement with the ALA Board included the following statement of purpose: "To encourage original creative work in the field of books for children. To emphasize to the public that contributions to the literature for children deserve similar recognition to poetry, plays, or novels. To give those librarians, who make it their life work to serve children's reading interests, an opportunity to encourage good writing in this field."

The medal is awarded by the Association for Library Service to Children, a division of the ALA. Other books on the final ballot for the Newbery are considered Newbery Honor Books.

In evaluating the candidates for exceptional children's literature, the committee members must consider the following criteria:

- The interpretation of the theme or concept
- Presentation of the information, including accuracy, clarity, and organization
- Development of plot
- Delineation of characters
- Delineation of setting
- Appropriateness of style
- Excellence of presentation for a child audience
- The book as a contribution to literature as a whole. The committee is to base its decision primarily on the text of the book, although other aspects of a book, such as illustrations or overall design, may be considered if they are an integral part of the story being conveyed.

Titles in

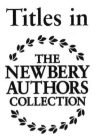

THE NEWBERY AUTHORS COLLECTION

THE
NEWBERY
AUTHORS
COLLECTION

For the Sake of Freedom

and Other Selections by Newbery Authors

Edited by Martin H. Greenberg
and Charles G. Waugh

Gareth Stevens Publishing
A WORLD ALMANAC EDUCATION GROUP COMPANY

The American Library Association receives a portion of the sale price of each volume in *The Newbery Authors Collection*.

The Newbery Medal was named for eighteenth-century British bookseller John Newbery. It is awarded annually by the Association for Library Service to Children, a division of the American Library Association, to the author of the most distinguished contribution to American literature for children. The American Library Association has granted the use of the Newbery name.

A note from the editors: These stories reflect many of the values, opinions, and standards of language that existed during the times in which the works were written. Much of the language is also a reflection of the personalities and lifestyles of the stories' narrators and characters. Readers today may strongly disagree, for example, with the ways in which members of various groups, such as women or ethnic minorities, are described. In compiling these works, however, we felt that it was important to capture as much of the flavor and character of the original stories as we could. Rather than delete or alter language that is intrinsically important to the literature, we hope that these stories will give parents, educators, and young readers a chance to think and talk about the many ways in which people lead their lives, view the world, and express their feelings about what they have lived through.

Please visit our web site at: www.garethstevens.com
For a free color catalog describing Gareth Stevens Publishing's list of high-quality books and multimedia programs, call 1-800-542-2595 (USA) or 1-800-461-9120 (Canada). Gareth Stevens Publishing's Fax: (414) 332-3567.

Library of Congress Cataloging-in-Publication Data available upon request from publisher. Fax: (414) 336-0157 for the attention of the Publishing Records Department.

ISBN 0-8368-2855-0

First published in 2001 by
Gareth Stevens Publishing
A World Almanac Education Group Company
330 West Olive Street, Suite 100
Milwaukee, WI 53212 USA

16.95

❧ Contents ❧

Edited by Martin H. Greenberg and Charles G. Waugh

For the Sake of Freedom

Will James

I was headed for wild horse country. I'd just ended up on a job of breaking a string of fine three and four year old colts for the Kant-Hook horse outfit, drawed my money, run in my private horses and was catered to my natural hankering to drift on and see new territory.

I'd often heard tell of a country a few hundred miles to the south, where there was not much else but wild horses and antelope, and some few cattle. It was a desert country, water miles apart, some of the springs was poisonous and many others dried up during summer months. On account of the land being covered with sharp lava and shale rock it was mighty hard on hoofs. Brush feed and scarce grama grass was like on the run, and the few cattle that ranged in that country kept sore-footed and poor by trying to catch up with it, and after a day and a night of rustling for feed, with very little rest in between, they'd hardly get their fill or rest when thirst would force them to hightail to the closest watering place, which would be miles away.

That was what I'd heard tell of that country, the wild horse country I was heading for. I'd been in many countries like it before and liked 'em well; there was lots of room and no fences and a feller appreciated shade and water more. It wasn't no cow country, and most of the cattle that run in there had just strayed and got to ranging there of their own accord. They'd be rounded up once or twice a year and then left free to range as they wished. It was open country all around and many of 'em would drift back.

But if that perticular country wasn't much fit for cattle the wild horse seemed to do well enough and accumulated there, and being they was on range where there was so few cattle, not many riders come to spoil their peace. Only once in a long while mustang runners would set up a water or blind trap and a few of the wild ones would be caught and shipped out of the territory. But the wild ones kept pretty well up to their numbers, and sometimes, as range horses would join the mustangs, that would help keep the numbers up to about the same, for the range horses would soon get as wild as the mustangs themselves.

The long distances between water and feed didn't bother the wild horses near as much as it did the cattle. They was foaled on hard ground and their hoofs growed to be as hard as the sharp lava rock that covered it. They was near as light on their feet as the antelope that run on that same range and, like the antelope, they'd been crowded out of surrounding countries by wire fences of farms and ranches till they come to that land that was of mighty little use to man for his cattle, and of no use at all for sheep.

Of course that land of the mustang and antelope could be used for the better bred range horse, but the mustang would have to be got rid of first, like has been done in many such places, and so the range horses wouldn't lose their breeding by mixing with the wild ones. The range horse runs as free on the range as the mustang does, only he's used to seeing a rider more often, he won't try very hard to get away, and will turn as the rider wishes or to where he points him, and on into a corral without causing much trouble. In the corral the unbroke range horse is near as wild as the mustang. When first caught he'll fight just as much, and when first rode he'll usually buck harder and longer than the mustang will.

The average range horse originates from the mustang, only he's been bred up as to size for different purposes with imported thoroughbreds and to where he's worth raising and branding. The brand identifies the horse as to who he belongs to, and there's still many branded range horses who show some of the old time mustang blood.

The wild horse goes unbranded, of course. He's just as hard to round up and corral as antelope or deer would be, and if a rider crowds a wild bunch to go to a certain place, that wild bunch will scatter all directions, like a bunch of quail. A strong, hidden corral has to be built to catch them, that's called a blind trap. A water trap is a corral in plain sight and around a spring, one wide gate is sprung on 'em. They'll usually travel a long ways to some other watering place rather than go inside a water trap to drink, for the wild horse is mighty wise, and suspicious of any enclosure.

There's usually no claim on the wild horse, and any man who catches one has got himself a horse free, but there's the catch.

From what's been handed down to me from old-time cow-boys who had the same handed down to them from other old-timers before them, and so on, back to the time when the first horses came to America, I get it that them horses was Arabians, and a Spaniard by the name of Cortez brought 'em over by boat from Spain and landed 'em in Old Mexico, where they accumulated and some of 'em got away, run wild and drifted North. Them Arabian horses is the ones our mustangs originated from. They was a wild and sort of inbred bunch but they saved many a man and Indian from walking.

What we call mustangs now days has very little of that old mustang breed. That's been mostly bred out of 'em by imported horses, and them that's now running wild are just mixed breeds of range horses that didn't get rounded up regular, and hit for wild country where they seldom see a rider. Like in that wild horse desert country I was headed for. I was two days' ride away from the outfit, where I'd finished up on my job of breaking horses, when I come to a fair-sized cow town. I stayed there a couple of days, got all cleaned up, hair cut and trimmings, supplied up on a pack horse load of grub, clothes and all such as I needed, celebrated a bit and then hit out of town early one morning, headed on for the wild horse country. I had six good horses with me. There was only two I hadn't broke to ride as yet, but I used 'em to pack, my grub supply was well tied down on one and the other hadn't been able to buck his pack off either. He was packing my bedding, extra clothes and warbag.

I was hazing my horses through a lane that led out of town a ways when I noticed two fresh horse tracks along the road, looked like only a couple of hours old on account I could see they was made after the night's dew fall had settled the dust.

The fresh stirred earth made by their tracks stood out plain. One of the horse's tracks was of a fair-sized saddle horse, I figured. He was shod. The other horse's track was of a smaller horse and barefooted.

I didn't pay much attention to the two fresh horses' tracks only to glance at 'em, as a feller naturally will. That's a kind of range rider's instinct, to notice all signs and tracks, for stock will stray and the information of such tracks to some owner who might be hunting for them would be helpful to him, sometimes helpful in many other ways. A feller can never tell.

Them horse tracks stayed on the road ahead of me for many miles after leaving the lane that led out of town. I thought at first that the shod horse was being rode, on account of his tracks keeping so straight ahead, but later I seen where he'd sort of checked up to nip at some grass. Then I knowed he was a loose horse, and not wasting much time on his way to wherever him and the barefooted one was headed.

A few miles further on, the tracks branched off the road on a trail that led to some rough hills. I kept my horses on the road which seemed to circle around them same rough hills and sort of forgot about the fresh tracks. But I would have remembered seeing them tracks if any rider had asked me about 'em.

And I did remember them well, for, quite a few days afterwards and about a hundred and fifty miles from where I'd first seen 'em, I run into them very same tracks again and I recognized 'em quick. This time the tracks interested me a heap more. Them two horses sure must be travelling, I thought, for I hadn't wasted no time myself, and they sure must know of one certain range they was hitting for and anxious to get there because, on their trail, they'd had to go through a couple of pretty thickly settled valleys and skirt around or go through one or two towns. Then there was a wide river they had to swim acrost. There was no bridge that I know of to within a hundred miles either way and I crossed my horses on a ferry.

Well, thinking of what places they went through to get to where they wanted to get sure set me to wonder at them two horses, and their tracks got to be more than interesting to me.

But if I wondered about them then, I got to wondering about 'em plenty more as I drifted on, for their tracks seemed to be leading right the way I was headed, towards the wild horse territory. From the time I run into their tracks again this second time I run into them some more as I rode on. They was hitting pretty well straight acrost country and taking short cuts on and off trails, where, with me, I'd stick to easier going and sort of circle around the roughest parts. I know that in their cross-country drifting they crossed rimrocked and box canyons where it'd bother a mountain goat to climb in and out of, and as days went on and I run into their tracks now and again I then got to hankering to catch with 'em. I could see by their tracks and signs that they was seldom very far ahead of me, and sometimes I expected to see them after topping some ridge or mountain pass. I wondered how come they drifted so straight and steady. They seemed to graze and water as they went, seldom stopping, and as they come to bunches of horses, as they did many times, the shod track showed where they didn't stop to mix in and graze a while, as most horses would, but went right on as though they was mighty anxious to get to wherever they was going.

One morning I was camped by the first railroad track I'd

seen since leaving the cow town about two hundred and fifty miles to the North. The railroad crossed a river there, and on account of high and solid rimrocks on both sides of the river, there was no way to get down and swim acrost or to get out on the other side. The only way to cross the river right at that place was on the railroad trestle and I sure wasn't going to take no chance of shoving my horses over that, they might get excited and jump in the river below or stick a leg and break it between the timbers of the trestle which was about three or four inches apart and allowed enough space for a hoof to go through.

There was only one way for me to go, that was either up or down the river till I come to a crossing or ferry or wagon bridge, and the going, either up or down that river looked plenty rough.

It was as I was sizing up the hills over my camp fire and by the sun's first rays that I got my first glimpse of the two horses that'd been making tracks ahead of me since I left the cow town. One was a bald-faced, stocking-legged black and the other was a bay filly. They both was good looking horses, specially while I was watching 'em, for they seemed excited as to finding a place to cross the river. They acted like they'd already been up and down it a few times looking for such a place, and when they come down off the hill and to the railroad they stopped, sniffed at the rails and then looked along the trestle, as if they would cross on that.

I was glad that my camp and horses was out of their sight because that might of scared 'em into crossing on the trestle. They trotted on down along the rim of the river and I figured they would find a place to cross down that way. But I'd just about got my outfit ready to pack, put out my fire and was going after my hobbled horses when I seen the two coming back, still on a trot and looking for a place to cross. They come to the railroad, stopped there and sized up the trestle again, more careful this time as if they figured that on the trestle was their only way to cross the river.

They didn't trot away from the trestle this time, they'd just wander a few yards and then come back to it. I watched 'em, feeling a little numb, because I knowed by their actions that they would try to cross that scary trestle.

They came to it once more, the black was in the lead, he lowered his head, snorted at the rails and timbers and made the first few steps on the start across. The filly was close by him.

I've witnessed some happenings that caused me to hold my breath but never any for so long a time as while watching them two horses crossing on that high and narrow trestle. I felt chilled and petrified and I don't think I could of moved if I wanted to or kept from watching the two horses. With heads low, bodies crouched and quivering, they snorted as they carefully made every step. One step gone wrong and there'd be a broken leg, or maybe two in the struggle to get free, and then maybe a fall into the swift river a hundred feet below.

As I watched I wished I had scared them away before they started acrost that trestle, but it was too late now. They went on, careful with every step, and as they got near the center of the trestle I was afraid they'd get scared at the height, the noise of the river below, the distance they still had to go, and turn to stampede back. That would of been their finish, either by broken legs or falling over the edge. And what if a train come along?

I think I'd given one of my horses right then just to see them two safe acrost the trestle and on solid earth on the other side. But as long as it seemed, it wasn't so very long when they got on the other side, then they let out a loud whistling snort at the spooky trestle they'd just crossed and hightailed it as fast as they could out of sight.

I rode up the river for a couple of days before I found a place to cross it, and as I rode I often wondered at the power of instinct to call free horses to cross such as the trestle which both was in dead fear of and which no amount of riders could of forced 'em to cross. It was the homing instinct of the wild horse that had called 'em, and I got proof of that some time later.

I'd got to the wild horse country I'd headed for. I'd found most of the scattered springs there had old dilapidated corrals around 'em, water traps. The wild horses had lost their suspicion of 'em and come right inside to water, and figuring on catching a few of them I located a little scope of country, high up where stock wouldn't naturally go and where feed was fairly good for my horses, and there I set up camp, about two miles from the closest spring, and went to work patching up the old corral at that spring so it would hold a bunch of wild ones when I sprung the gate on 'em. It wasn't a regular trap gate, just a swinging gate, but I fixed it so it would swing well, tied a long rope to it so that when pulled it would close the gate fast and tight. I dug me a pit as far as the long rope would reach, covered it up with brush and dirt, leaving only a hole big enough for me to crawl in and out, and I was ready for the wild ones to come.

But I didn't want to use that trap yet. I moved camp to another spring about thirty miles away and fixed another old trap there the same as I did the first, then I came back to the first trap and by that time the signs I'd made in fixing it had been pretty well blown over, and I noticed by tracks that quite a few bunches had come to water there.

My camp set up again, I went to the trap about sundown and got settled in my pit for the night, but no horses came that night nor the next, but the third night was good, a bunch came in. I counted eight head against the skyline and I pulled the gate slambang on the last one's tail as he went in.

The corral held 'em, and the next day I roped and throwed every one of 'em, tied a front foot to the tail with just enough rope so the foot only touched the ground and was useless for any fast travelling. All the wild ones fixed up that way I went and got my saddle horses, packed up my outfit and brought all down to turn in with the wild ones, and then opened the corral gate and started out.

Being alone I had to do some tall riding to keep all the horses together but the wild ones couldn't get away with a front foot being held back, and when about four or five miles from the trap, they finally settled down to follow my saddle horses.

On account of the mustangs having one foot tied up I could only drive 'em about fifteen miles the first day. There was no water in that distance and the horses was thirsty, so I changed saddle horses and rode all night as I let the horses graze and drift on slow. It was high noon the next day when I come to a spring and there I cooked myself a bait and let the horses rest close to water the whole afternoon. When night come and it

16

got cooler I started 'em on the move again, found water late the next day and in a corral close by I took the foot ropes off the mustangs. They was well "herd-broke" by then. That is, they would turn the way I wanted 'em and stay in one bunch, with my saddle horses.

I'd drove the horses about six days from the time I left the trap when I come to a big settled valley. In a lane leading to the town I met a rider who helped me drive the horses to the shipping yards on the outskirts of the town, and I sold 'em there the next day for eight dollars a head, a fair price for mustangs in that country.

My saddle horses rested up some, I headed back to the wild horse country. I used the second trap this time. Mustangs get suspicious quick if one trap is used often. I caught only a small bunch, six head, but being I had no way of keeping 'em till I caught another bunch, I took 'em in. They was all grown stuff and brought me ten dollars a head.

I think I caught and took in three more bunches after that. I remember there was fourteen head in one of the bunches I took in.

Fall was coming on, but the wild horse country was still hot and dry and I wanted to catch another bunch before a rain come, leaving plenty of water everwhere and making my traps useless.

I was at one of my traps early one evening. The sun hadn't gone down yet and I was enjoying a smoke by the shade of the corral when I seen two wild ones coming. I could tell they was thirsty because they was coming on a trot. I didn't want to bother with catching only two, but I didn't want to keep them from drinking, and I crawled into my pit without first investigating if rattlers or tarantulers had crawled in there, as they sometimes would.

The horses, always suspicious of a water trap, even if it hadn't been used for years, slowed up when they come within a few hundred yards of it and snorted and sniffed as they carefully came closer. It was then that I recognized the two horses. They was the two that had trailed ahead of me for over four hundred miles from the North. They was now on their home range and the reason I hadn't seen 'em before is that they'd been watering at other places in the wild horse country.

As I said before, I didn't want to bother with catching only two horses, and when them two came in the trap, and after they'd drank some, I somehow couldn't help but slam the gate closed on 'em. They were surprised, of course, as the gate slammed and they tore around some, but they soon quieted down again, and with a short of hopeless look came to a standstill. They'd been caught before and they seemed to realize mighty well that their freedom was lost once again.

I got out of the pit and climbed into the corral. They only stood and quivered and snorted, and as I watched 'em I noticed that the black horse had wore his shoes off, but he had a little spot on his back that would never wear off, that was a saddle mark.

As usual when inside the trap I had my rope in my hand, and to get better acquainted with the black horse I made a loop and flipped it over his head. As I'd already figured long before, he was a broke horse and he didn't try to break away when I caught him. Instead he turned and faced me and only snorted a little as I pulled on the rope and led him up to me. He was gentle and whoever had broke him had not broke his spirit. He was still the wild horse at heart, and if free again in his home range he now was in, he'd be harder to catch than the other wild ones which had never been caught. He'd be wiser and harder to get into traps. It was nothing against his wisdom that he'd been caught in my trap because it was old and sure looked desolated.

The black was far better built than the average wild horse in that country. He was good size too, and I judged him to be only about six years old. A good horse, and I figured I could sell him for near as much as I could get for any ten head of average wild ones I could catch there. The filly was good too, but fillies don't count much in the wild horse country.

I decided to keep the two horses. I went to where I'd hid my saddled horse in the brush and rode to my camp where I crawled into my regular bed. Night had come but I didn't go to sleep for a long time, I got to thinking of the two horses in the trap, and as I did it came to me how much their freedom and home range meant to them. They'd run away from a country of plenty grass, shade and water, where they'd been well taken care of. Their condition proved that. Then they'd drifted acrost rough countries, through lanes and settlements every wild horse fears, swam rivers and even crossed on that scary trestle, all to get back to a desert and barren dry country. But that was their range, and wild freedom was there.

I thought again and again of their crossing that strange and spooky railroad trestle to get to that home range of theirs, and now, after only a short while of freedom they was in a trap again, and I'd closed the gate on 'em. I'd took away the freedom they'd risked so much to get back to.

The stars blinked down at me. I set up and rolled me a

Will James

smoke and, still thinking of the two horses in the trap, it struck me kind of queer when it come to me of a sudden that there was nothing to stop me from opening that trap gate and giving the horses their freedom again. That thought seemed to relieve me a considerable. I finished my cigarette and then went right to sleep, all peaceful.

Who'd ever heard of wild horse hunter turning horses loose after he'd caught 'em? Such a thing is never thought of. As I rode down to the trap I got to thinking as I did the night before that a couple of horses more or less sure wouldn't make much difference to me, and whatever money they'd bring wouldn't mean so much either, not near as much as the pleasure of seeing them go free.

Besides, I had plenty enough money. I didn't need no new saddle and the rest of my outfit was good for plenty more wear, then I had a string of mighty good saddle horses and there was thousands of miles of range country. What more could a cowboy want?

But I was kind of cheated in the pleasure of carrying out my plans, for as I got to the trap I seen it was empty. Them two daggone horses had found a hole in the trap, they'd made it bigger and squeezed through.

Well, I thought, it was good thing they got away because I might of changed my mind. I looked down the big desert flat and couldn't even see their dust nowhere. I grinned as I thought how wise they was and how hard they'd be to trap again.

I patched the hole in the trap, figuring on catching one more bunch of wild ones before leaving that country. For I was again hankering for new range. I stayed in the pit two nights. No horses came, then big clouds piled up fast during the third

20

afternoon, seemed like from nowhere, and I hardly felt the first few raindrops when whole sheets of it came, soaking me through.

It seldom rained in that desert, but when it did that time it didn't come down by drops but more by bucketfuls. In a short time every little dry wash was a roaring river, boulders was washed away like grains of sand, and from the high knoll I'd rode up onto I seen my trap washed away like it was made of toothpicks.

The cloudburst didn't last long, only about an hour, but it had sure moved a lot of country in that time. It was like big dams had broke loose from everywhere at once, and the big hardpan flats which was sizzling hot a few hours before was now transformed into big lakes. Plenty of water for the wild ones now, I thought, and they wouldn't be coming to water traps to drink for some weeks. By then more rain would most likely come, for winter wasn't far away.

The country sure looked clean and fresh and smelled good as the sun came up the next morning. It gave me the good feeling to ramble on over it, and as I boiled my coffee I got to thinking of another country I'd heard tell of and which I'd never seen. It was located some few hundred miles further on south, and as winter was coming on I figured the mild climate wouldn't go bad, for a spell anyway.

And You Wonder Why We Get Called the Weird Watsons

Christopher Paul Curtis

It was one of those super-duper-cold Saturdays. One of those days that when you breathed out your breath kind of hung frozen in the air like a hunk of smoke and you could walk along and look exactly like a train blowing out big, fat, white puffs of smoke.

It was so cold that if you were stupid enough to go outside your eyes would automatically blink a thousand times all by themselves, probably so the juice inside of them wouldn't freeze up. It was so cold that if you spit, the slob would be an ice cube before it hit the ground. It was about a zillion degrees below zero.

It was even cold inside our house. We put sweaters and hats and scarves and three pairs of socks on and still were cold. The thermostat was turned all the way up and the furnace was banging and sounding like it was about to blow up but it still felt like Jack Frost had moved in with us.

All of my family sat real close together on the couch under a blanket. Dad said this would generate a little heat but he didn't have to tell us this, it seemed like the cold automatically made us want to get together and huddle up. My little sister, Joetta, sat in the middle and all you could see were her eyes because she had a scarf wrapped around her head. I was next to her, and on the outside was my mother.

Momma was the only one who wasn't born in Flint so the cold was coldest to her. All you could see were her eyes too, and they were shooting bad looks at Dad. She always blamed him for bringing her all the way from Alabama to Michigan, a state she called a giant icebox. Dad was bundled up on the other side of Joey, trying to look at anything but Momma. Next to Dad, sitting with a little space between them, was my older brother, Byron.

Byron had just turned thirteen so he was officially a teenage juvenile delinquent and didn't think it was "cool" to touch any-body or let anyone touch him, even if it meant he froze to death. Byron had tucked the blanket between him and Dad down into the cushion of the couch to make sure he couldn't be touched.

Dad turned on the TV to try to make us forget how cold we were but all that did was get him in trouble. There was a spe-cial news report on Channel 12 telling about how bad the weather was and Dad groaned when the guy said, "If you think it's cold now, wait until tonight, the temperature is expected to drop into record-low territory, possibly reaching the negative twenties! In fact, we won't be seeing anything above zero for the next four to five days!" He was smiling when he said this but none of the Watson family thought it was funny. We all looked over at Dad. He just shook his head and pulled the blanket over his eyes.

Then the guy on TV said, "Here's a little something we can

use to brighten our spirits and give us some hope for the future: The temperature in Atlanta, Georgia, is forecast to reach . . . " Dad coughed real loud and jumped off the couch to turn the TV off but we all heard the weatherman say, ". . . the mid-seventies!" The guy might as well have tied Dad to a tree and said, "Ready, aim, fire!"

"Atlanta!" Momma said. "That's a hundred and fifty miles from home!"

"Wilona . . . ," Dad said.

"I knew it," Momma said. "I knew I should have listened to Moses Henderson!"

"Who?" I asked.

Dad said, "Oh Lord, not that sorry story. You've got to let me tell about what happened with him."

Momma said, "There's not a whole lot to tell, just a story about a young girl who made a bad choice. But if you do tell it, make sure you get all the facts right."

We all huddled as close as we could get because we knew Dad was going to try to make us forget about being cold by cutting up. Me and Joey started smiling right away, and Byron tried to look cool and bored.

"Kids," Dad said, "I almost wasn't your father. You guys came real close to having a clown for a daddy named Hambone Henderson. . . ."

"Daniel Watson, you stop right there. You're the one who started that 'Hambone' nonsense. Before you started that everyone called him his Christian name, Moses. And he was a respectable boy too, he wasn't a clown at all."

"But the name stuck, didn't it? Hambone Henderson. Me and your granddaddy called him that because the boy had a

24

AND YOU WONDER WHY WE GET CALLED THE WEIRD WATSONS

head shaped just like a hambone, had more knots and bumps on his head than a dinosaur. So as you guys sit here giving me these dirty looks because it's a little chilly outside ask yourselves if you'd rather be a little cool or go through life being known as the Hambonettes."

Me and Joey cracked up, Byron kind of chuckled and Momma put her hand over her mouth. She did this whenever she was going to give a smile because she had a great big gap between her front teeth. If Momma thought something was funny, first you'd see her trying to keep her lips together to hide the gap, then, if the smile got to be too strong, you'd see the gap for a hot second before Momma's hand would come up to cover it, then she'd crack up too.

Laughing only encouraged Dad to cut up more, so when he saw the whole family thinking he was funny he really started putting on a show.

He stood in front of the TV. "Yup, Hambone Henderson proposed to your mother around the same time I did. Fought dirty too, told your momma a pack of lies about me and when she didn't believe them he told her a pack of lies about Flint."

Dad started talking Southern-style, imitating this Hambone guy. "Wilona, I heard tell about the weather up that far north in Flint, Mitch-again, heard it's colder than inside a icebox. Seen a movie about it, think it was made in Flint. Movie called *Nanook of the North*. Yup, do believe for sure it was made in Flint. Uh-huh, Flint, Mitch-again.

"Folks there live in these things called igloos. According to what I seen in this here movie most the folks in Flint is Chinese. Don't believe I seen nan one colored person in the whole dang city. You a 'Bama gal, don't believe you'd be too happy living in no igloo. Ain't got nothing against 'em, but don't believe you'd be too happy living 'mongst a whole slew of Chinese folks. Don't believe you'd like the food. Only thing them Chinese folks in that movie et was whales and seals. Don't believe you'd like no whale meat. Don't taste a lick like chicken. Don't taste like pork at all."

Momma pulled her hand away from her mouth. "Daniel Watson, you are one lying man! Only thing you said that was true was that being in Flint is like living in a igloo. I knew I should have listened to Moses. Maybe these babies mighta been born with lumpy heads but at least they'da had *warm* lumpy heads!

"You know Birmingham is a good place, and I don't mean just the weather either. The life is slower, the people are friendlier—"

"Oh yeah," Dad interrupted, "they're a laugh a minute down there. Let's see, where was that 'Coloreds Only' bathroom downtown?"

"Daniel, you know what I mean, things aren't perfect but people are more honest about the way they feel"—she took her mean eyes off Dad and put them on Byron—"and folks there do know how to respect their parents."

Byron rolled his eyes like he didn't care. All he did was tuck the blanket farther into the couch's cushion.

Dad didn't like the direction the conversation was going so he called the landlord for the hundredth time. The phone was still busy.

"That snake in the grass has got his phone off the hook. Well, it's going to be too cold to stay here tonight, let me call Cydney. She just had that new furnace put in, maybe we can spend the night there." Aunt Cydney was kind of mean but her house was always warm so we kept our fingers crossed that she was home.

Everyone, even Byron, cheered when Dad got Aunt Cydney and she told us to hurry over before we froze to death.

Dad went out to try and get the Brown Bomber started. That was what we called our car. It was a 1948 Plymouth that was dull brown and real big, Byron said it was turd brown. Uncle Bud gave it to Dad when it was thirteen years old and we'd had it for two years. Me and Dad took real good care of it but some of the time it didn't like to start up in the winter.

After five minutes Dad came back in huffing and puffing and slapping his arms across his chest.

"Well, it was touch and go for a while, but the Great Brown One pulled through again!" Everyone cheered, but me and Byron quit cheering and started frowning right away. By the way Dad smiled at us we knew what was coming next. Dad pulled two ice scrapers out of his pocket and said, "O.K., boys, let's get out there and knock those windows out."

We moaned and groaned and put some more coats on and went outside to scrape the car's windows. I could tell by the way he was pouting that Byron was going to try and get out of doing his share of the work.

"I'm not going to do your part, Byron, you'd better do it and I'm not playing either."

"Shut up, punk."

I went over to the Brown Bomber's passenger side and started hacking away at the scab of ice that was all over the windows. I finished Momma's window and took a break. Scraping ice off of windows when it's that cold can kill you!

I didn't hear any sound coming from the other side of the car so I yelled out, "I'm serious, Byron, I'm not doing that side too, and I'm only going to do half the windshield, I don't care what you do to me." The windshield on the Bomber wasn't like the new 1963 cars, it had a big bar running down the middle of it, dividing it in half.

"Shut your stupid mouth, I got something more important to do right now."

I peeked around the back of the car to see what By was up to. The only thing he'd scraped off was the outside mirror and he was bending down to look at himself in it. He saw me and said, "You know what, square? I must be adopted, there just ain't no way two folks as ugly as your momma and daddy coulda give birth to someone as sharp as me!"

He was running his hands over his head like he was brushing his hair.

I said, "Forget you," and went back over to the other side of the car to finish the back window. I had half of the ice off when I had to stop again and catch my breath. I heard Byron mumble my name.

I said, "You think I'm stupid? It's not going to work this time." He mumbled my name again. It sounded like his mouth was full of something. I knew this was a trick, I knew this was going to be How to Survive a Blizzard, Part Two.

How to Survive a Blizzard, Part One had been last night when I was outside playing in the snow and Byron and his buddy, Buphead, came walking by. Buphead has officially been a juvenile delinquent even longer than Byron.

"Say, kid," By had said, "you wanna learn somethin' that might save your stupid life one day?"

I should have known better, but I was bored and I think maybe the cold weather was making my brain slow, so I said, "What's that?"

"We gonna teach you how to survive a blizzard."

"How?"

Byron put his hands in front of his face and said, "This is the most important thing to remember, O.K.?"

"Why?"

"Well, first we gotta show you what it feels like to be trapped in a blizzard. You ready?" He whispered something to Buphead and they both laughed.

"I'm ready."

I should have known that the only reason Buphead and By would want to play with me was to do something mean.

"O.K.," By said, "first thing you gotta worry about is high winds."

Byron and Buphead each grabbed one of my arms and one of my legs and swung me between them going, "*Wooo*, blizzard warnings! Blizzard warnings! *Wooo!* Take cover!"

Buphead counted to three and on the third swing they let me go in the air. I landed headfirst in a snowbank.

But that was O.K. because I had on three coats, two sweaters, a T-shirt, three pairs of pants and four socks along with a scarf, a hat and a hood. These guys couldn't have hurt me if they'd thrown me off the Empire State Building!

After I climbed out of the snowbank they started laughing and so did I.

"Cool, Baby Bruh," By said, "you passed that part of the test with a B-plus, what do you think, Buphead?"

Buphead said, "Yeah, I'd give the little punk a A."

They whispered some more and started laughing again.

"O.K.," By said, "second thing you gotta learn is how to keep your balance in a high wind. You gotta be good at this so you don't get blowed into no polar bear dens."

They put me in between them and started making me spin round and round, it seemed like they spun me for about half an hour. When slob started flying out of my mouth they let me stop and I wobbled around for a while before they pushed me back in the same snowbank.

When everything stopped going in circles I got up and we all laughed again.

They whispered some more and then By said, "What you think, Buphead? He kept his balance a good long time, I'm gonna give him a A-minus."

"I ain't as hard a grader as you, I'ma give the little punk a double A-minus."

"O.K., Kenny, now the last part of Surviving a Blizzard, you ready?"

"Yup!"

"You passed the wind test and did real good on the balance test but now we gotta see if you ready to graduate. You remember what we told you was the most important part about survivin'?"

"Yup!"

"O.K., here we go. Buphead, tell him 'bout the final exam."

Buphead turned me around to look at him, putting my back to Byron. "O.K., square," he started, "I wanna make sure you ready for this one, you done so good so far I wanna make sure you don't blow it at graduation time. You think you ready?"

I nodded, getting ready to be thrown in the snowbank real hard this time. I made up my mind I wasn't going to cry or anything, I made up my mind that no matter how hard they threw me in that snow I was going to get up laughing.

"O.K.," Buphead said, "everything's cool, you 'member what your brother said about puttin' your hands up?"

"Like this?" I covered my face with my gloves.

"Yeah, that's it!" Buphead looked over my shoulder at Byron and then said, "*Wooo!* High winds, blowing snow! *Wooo!* Look out! Blizzard a-comin'! Death around the corner! Look out!"

Byron mumbled my name and I turned around to see why his voice sounded so funny. As soon as I looked at him Byron blasted me in the face with a mouthful of snow.

Man! It was hard to believe how much stuff By could put in his mouth! Him and Buphead just about died laughing as I stood there with snow and spit and ice dripping off my face.

Byron caught his breath and said, "Aww, man, you flunked! You done so good, then you go and flunk the Blowin' Snow section of How to Survive a Blizzard, you forgot to put your hands up! What you say, Buphead, F?"

"Yeah, double F-minus!"

It was a good thing my face was numb from the cold already or I might have froze to death. I was too embarrassed about getting tricked to tell on them so I went in the house and watched TV.

So as me and By scraped the ice off the Brown Bomber I wasn't going to get fooled again. I kept on chopping ice off the back window and ignored By's mumbling voice.

The next time I took a little rest Byron was still calling my name but sounding like he had something in his mouth. He was saying. "Keh-ee! Keh-ee! Hel' . . . hel' . . . !" When he started banging on the door of the car I went to take a peek at what was going on.

By was leaned over the outside mirror, looking at something in it real close. Big puffs of steam were coming out of the side of the mirror.

I picked up a big, hard chunk of ice to get ready for Byron's trick.

"Keh-ee! Keh-ee! Hel' me! Hel' me! Go geh Momma! Go geh Mom-ma! Huwwy uh!"

"I'm not playing, Byron! I'm not that stupid! You'd better start doing your side of the car or I'll tear you up with this ice-ball."

He banged his hand against the car harder and started stomping his feet. "Oh, please, Keh-ee! Hel' me, go geh Mom-ma!"

I raised the ice chunk over my head. "I'm not playing, By, you better get busy or I'm telling Dad."

I moved closer and when I got next to him I could see boogers running out of his nose and tears running down his cheeks. These weren't tears from the cold either, these were big juicy crybaby tears! I dropped my ice chunk.

"By! What's wrong?"

"Hel' me! Keh-ee! Go geh hel'!"

I moved closer. I couldn't believe my eyes! Byron's mouth was frozen on the mirror! He was as stuck as a fly on flypaper!

I could have done a lot of stuff to him. If it had been me with my lips stuck on something like this he'd have tortured me for a couple of days before he got help. Not me, though, I nearly broke my neck trying to get into the house to rescue Byron.

As soon as I ran through the front door Momma, Dad and Joey all yelled, "Close that door!"

"Momma, quick! It's By! He's froze up outside!"

No one seemed too impressed.

I screamed, "Really! He's froze to the car! Help! He's crying!"

That shook them up. You could cut Byron's head off and he probably wouldn't cry.

"Kenneth Bernard Watson, what on earth are you talking about?"

"Momma, please hurry up!"

Momma, Dad and Joey threw on some extra coats and followed me to the Brown Bomber.

The fly was still stuck and buzzing. "Oh, Mom-ma! Hel' me! Get me offa 'ere!"

"Oh my Lord!" Momma screamed, and I thought she was going to do one of those movie-style faints, she even put her hand over her forehead and staggered back a little bit.

Joey, of course, started crying right along with Byron.

Dad was doing his best not to explode laughing. Big puffs of smoke were coming out of his nose and mouth as he tried to squeeze his laughs down. Finally he put his head on his arms and leaned against the car's hood and howled.

"Byron," Momma said, gently wiping tears off his cheeks with the end of her scarf, "it's O.K., sweetheart, how'd this happen?" She sounded like she was going to be crying in a minute herself.

Dad raised his head and said, "Why are you asking how it

happened? Can't you tell, Wilona? This little knucklehead was kissing his reflection in the mirror and got his lips stuck!" Dad took a real deep breath. "Is your tongue stuck too?"

"No! Quit teasin', Da-ee! Hel'! Hel'!"

"Well, at least the boy hadn't gotten too passionate with himself!" Dad thought that was hilarious and put his head back on his arms.

Momma didn't see anything funny. "Daniel Watson! What are we gonna do? What do y'all do when this happens up he-uh?" Momma started talking Southern-style when she got worried. Instead of saying "here" she said "he-uh" and instead of saying "you all" she said "y'all."

Daddy stopped laughing long enough to say, "Wilona, I've lived in Flint all my life, thirty-five years, and I swear this is the first time I've ever seen anyone with their lips frozen to a mirror. Honey, I don't know what to do, wait till he thaws out?"

"Pull him off, Dad," I suggested. Byron went nuts! He started banging his hands on the Brown Bomber's doors again and mumbling, "No! No! Mom-ma, doe leh him!"

Joey blubbered out, "This is just like that horrible story Kenny read me about that guy Nar-sissy who stared at himself so long he forgot to eat and starved to death. Mommy, please save him!" She went over and hugged her arms around stupid Byron's waist.

Momma asked Dad, "What about hot water? Couldn't we pour enough hot water on the mirror so it would warm up and he could get off?" She kept wiping tears off By's cheeks and said, "Don't you worry, Baby, we gonna get you off of this." But her voice was so shaky and Southern that I wondered if we'd be driving around in the summer with a skeleton dangling from the outside mirror by its lips.

Dad said, "I don't know, pouring water on him might be the worst thing to do, but it might be our only chance. Why don't you go get some hot tap water and I'll stay to wipe his cheeks."

Joey told By, "Don't worry, we'll come right back." She stood on her tiptoes and gave By a kiss, then she and Momma ran inside. Dad cracked up all over again.

"Well, lover boy, I guess this means no one can call you Hot Lips, can they?"

Dad was killing himself. "Or the Last of the Red Hot Lovers either, huh?" He tugged on Byron's ear a little, pulling his face back.

By went nuts again. "Doe do dat! Mom-ma! Mom-ma, hel'! Keh-ee, go geh Mom-ma! Huwwy!"

"Hmm, I guess that's not going to work, is it?"

Every time he wiped away the tears and the little mustache of boogers on Byron's lip Dad couldn't help laughing, until a little river of tears was coming out of his eyes too.

Dad tried to straighten his face out when Momma and Joey came running back with a steaming glass of hot water, but the tears were still running down his cheeks.

Momma tried to pour water on the mirror but her hands were shaking so much, she was splashing it all over the place. Dad tried too, but he couldn't look at Byron without laughing and shaking.

That meant I had to do it.

I knew that if my lips were frozen on something and everybody was shaking too much to pour water on them except for Byron he'd do some real cruel stuff to me. He probably would have "accidentally" splashed my eyes until they were frozen open or put water in my ears until I couldn't hear anything, but not me. I gently poured a little stream of water over the mirror.

Dad was right! This was the worst thing we could do! The water made a cracking sound and froze solid as soon as it touched the mirror and By's lips!

Maybe By's mouth was frozen but his hands sure weren't and he popped me right in the forehead. Hard! I hate to say it but I started crying too.

It's no wonder the neighbors called us the Weird Watsons behind our backs. There we were, all five of us standing around a car with the temperature about a million degrees below zero and each and every one of us crying!

"'top! 'top!" By yelled.

"Daniel Watson, what're we gonna do?" Momma went nuts. "You gotta get this boy to the hospital! My baby is gonna die!"

Dad tried to look serious real quick.

"Wilona, how far do you think I'd get driving down the street with this little clown attached to the mirror? What am I supposed to do, have him run beside the car all the way down to the emergency room?"

Momma looked real close at By's mouth, closed her eyes for a second like she was praying and finally said, "Daniel, you get in there and call the hospital and see what they say we should do. Joey and Kenny, go with your daddy."

Dad and Joey went crying into the house. I stayed by the Brown Bomber. I figured Momma was clearing everybody out for something. Byron did too and looked at Momma in a real nervous way.

Momma put her scarf around Byron's face and said, "Sweetheart, you know we gotta do something. I'ma try to warm your face up a little. Just relax."

"O.K., Mom-ma."

"You know I love you and wouldn't do anything to hurt you, right?" If Momma was trying to make Byron relax she wasn't doing a real good job at it. All this talk about love and not getting hurt was making him real nervous.

"Wah are you gonna do? Huh? Doe hur' me! Keh-ee, hel'!"

Momma moved the scarf away and put one hand on Byron's chin and the other one on his forehead.

"No! Hel'! Hel' me, Keh-ee!"

Momma gave Byron's head a good hard snatch and my eyes automatically shut and my hands automatically flew up to cover my ears and my mouth automatically flew open and screamed out, "Yeeeowwwww!"

I didn't see it, but I bet Byron's lips stretched a mile before they finally let go of that mirror. I bet his lips looked like a giant rubber band before they snapped away from that glass!

I didn't hear it, but I bet Byron's lips made a sound like a giant piece of paper being ripped in half!

When I opened my eyes Byron was running to the house with his hands over his mouth and Momma following right behind him. I ran over to the mirror to see how much of Byron's mouth was stuck there.

The dirty dogs let Byron get away with not doing his share of the windows and I had to do the whole car myself. When we were finally going to Aunt Cydney's house I decided to pay Byron back for punching me in the forehead and getting out of doing his part of the window scraping. Joey was sitting between us so I felt kind of safe. I said to her, loud, "Joetta, guess what. I'm thinking about writing my own comic book."

"What about?"

"Well, it's going to be about this real mean criminal who has a terrible accident that turns him into a superhero."

Joey knew I was going to tease Byron so she sat there looking like I should be careful what I said. Finally I asked her, "Do you want to know what I'm going to call this new superhero?"

"What?"

"I'm going to call him the Lipless Wonder. All he does is beat up superheroes smaller than him and the only thing he's afraid of is a cold mirror!"

All the Weird Watsons except Byron cracked up. Momma's hand even covered her mouth. I was the only one who saw Byron flip me a dirty finger sign and try to whisper without smearing all the Vaseline Momma had put on his lips, "You wait, I'm gonna kick your little behind." Then he made his eyes go crossed, which was his favorite way of teasing me, but I didn't care, I knew who had won this time!

The Rascal Crow

Lloyd Alexander

Medwyn, ancient guardian and protector of animals, one day sent urgent word for the birds and beasts to join in council with him. So from lair and burrow, nest and hive, proud stag and humble mole, bright-winged eagle and drab wren, they hastened to his valley. No human could have found or followed the secret path to this shelter, for only creatures of field and forest had knowledge of it.

There they gathered, every kind and degree, one from each clan and tribe. Before them stood Medwyn garbed in a coarse brown robe, his white beard reaching to his waist, his white hair about his shoulders, his only ornament a golden band, set with a blue gem, circling his weathered brow. He spread his gnarled and knotted arms in welcome to the waiting council.

"You know, all of you," he began, in a clear voice unweakened by his years, "long ago, when the dark waters flooded Prydain, I built a ship and carried your forefathers here to safety. Now I must warn you: your own lives are threatened."

Hearing this, the animals murmured and twittered in dismay. But Kadwyr the crow flapped his glossy wings, clacked his beak, and gaily called out:

"What, more wind and water? Let the ducks have the joy of it! Don't worry about me. My nest is high and strong enough. I'll stay where I am. Good sailing to all web-feet!"

Chuckling, making loud, impudent quackings at the blue teal, Kadwyr would have flown off then and there. Medwyn summoned him back, saying:

"Ah, Kadwyr, you're as great a scamp as your grandsire who sailed with me. No, it is neither flood nor storm. The danger is far worse. King Arawn, Lord of the Land of Death, seeks to enslave all you forest creatures, to break you to his will and bind you to serve his evil ends. Those cousins to the eagles, the gentle gwythaints, have already fallen prey to him. Arawn has lured them to his realm and trapped them in iron cages. Alas, they are beyond our help. We can only grieve for them.

"Take warning from their fate," Medwyn continued. "For now the Death-Lord sends his Chief Huntsman to bait and snare you, to bring you captive to the Land of Death or to slaughter you without mercy. Together you must set your plans to stand against him."

"A crow's a match for any hunter," said Kadwyr. "Watch your step, the rest of you, especially you slow-footed cud-chewers."

Medwyn sighed and shook his head at the brash crow. "Even you, Kadwyr, may be glad for another's help."

Kadwyr only shrugged his wings and cocked a bold eye at Edyrnion the eagle, who flew to perch on Medwyn's outstretched arm.

"Friend of eagles," Edyrnion said, "I and my kinsmen will

keep watch from the sky. Our eyes are keen, our wings are swift. At first sight of the hunter, we will spread the alarm."

"Mind you, don't fly too close to the sun," put in Kadwyr with a raucous chuckle. "You'll singe your pinfeathers and molt ahead of season. If there's any watching needed, I'd best be the one to do it. I hear you're going a bit nearsighted these days."

The nimble crow hopped away before the eagle could call him to account for his teasing. And now the gray wolf Brynach came to crouch at Medwyn's feet, saying:

"Friend of wolves, I and my kinsmen will range the forest. Our teeth are sharp, our jaws are strong. Should the hunter come among us, let him beware of our wolf packs."

"And you'd better watch out for that long tail of yours," said Kadwyr. "With all your dashing back and forth, you're likely to get burrs in it. In fact, you might do well to leave all that roving and roaming to me. My beak's as sharp as any wolf's tooth. And," the crow added, winking, "I never have to stop and scratch fleas."

The wolf's golden eyes flashed and he looked ready to teach the crow a lesson in manners. But he kept his temper and sat back on his haunches as Gwybeddin the gnat flew close to Medwyn's ear and bravely piped up:

"Friend of gnats! We are a tiny folk, but we mean to do our best in any way we can."

Hearing this, Kadwyr squawked with laughter and called out to the gnat:

"Is that you, Prince Flyspeck? I can hardly see you. Listen, old friend, the best thing you can do is hide in a dust cloud, and no hunter will ever find you. Why, even your words are bigger than you are!"

Kadwyr's remarks so embarrassed the poor gnat that he blushed and buzzed away as fast as he could. Meantime, Nedir the spider had clambered up to Medwyn's sleeve, where she clung with her long legs, and declared:

"Friend of spiders! We spinners and weavers are craftsmen, not fighters. But we shall give our help gladly wherever it is needed."

"Take my advice, Granny," Kadwyr said with a chuckle, "and keep to your knitting. Be careful you don't get your arms and legs mixed up, or you'll never untangle them."

Kadwyr hopped about and flirted his tail feathers, croaking and cackling as the other creatures came forward one by one. The owl declared that he and his fellows would serve as night watch. The fox vowed to use his cunning to baffle the hunter and lead him on false trails. The bees pledged to wield their stings as swords and daggers. The bears offered their strength, the stags their speed, and the badgers their courage to protect their neighbors and themselves.

Last of all, plodding under his heavy burden, came Crugan-Crawgan the turtle.

"Friend of turtles," began Crugan-Crawgan in a halting voice, pondering each word, "I came . . . yes, well, that is to say I, ah, started . . . in all possible haste . . ."

"And we'll be well into next week by the time you've done telling us," Kadwyr said impatiently.

"We are . . . as I should be the first to admit . . . we are, alas, neither swift not strong. But if I might be allowed. . .ah, permitted to state . . . we're solid. Very, very . . . solid. And . . . steady."

"Have done!" cried Kadwyr, hopping onto the turtle's shell. "You'll put me to sleep! The safest thing you can do is stay locked up in that portable castle of yours. Pull in your head! Tuck in your tail! I'll see to it the hunter doesn't batter down your walls. By the way, old fellow, didn't you have a race with a snail the other day? Tell me, who won?"

"Oh, that," replied Crugan-Crawgan. "Yes, Kadwyr, you see, what happened . . ."

Kadwyr did not wait for the turtle's answer, for Medwyn now declared the council ended, and the crow flapped away, laughing and cackling to himself. "Gnats and spiders! Turtles! What an army! I'll have to keep an eye on all of them."

Once in the forest, however, Kadwyr gave little thought to Medwyn's warning. The beavers toiled at making their dams into strongholds; the squirrels stopped up the crannies in their hollow trees; the moles dug deeper tunnels and galleries. Though every creature offered him shelter in case of need, Kadwyr shook his glossy head and answered:

"Not for me, those holes and burrows! Wits and wings! Wings and wits! There's not a crow hatched who can't get the best of any hunter!"

Soon Edyrnion and his eagle kinsmen came swooping into the forest, beating their wings and spreading the alarm. The wolf packs leaped from their lairs, the bears from their dens, the foxes from their earths, gathering to join battle against the hunter; and all the forest dwellers, each in his own way, made ready to defend nest and bower, cave and covert.

Kadwyr, however, perched on a branch, rocking back and forth, whistling gaily, daring the invader to catch him. While the smaller, weaker animals hid silent and fearful, Kadwyr hopped up and down, cawing at the top of his voice. And before the crow knew it, the hunter sprang from a thicket.

Garbed in the skins of slain animals, a long knife at his belt, a bow and quiver of arrows slung over his shoulder, the hunter had come so stealthily that Kadwyr scarcely had a moment to collect his wits. The hunter flung out a net so strong and finely woven that once caught in it, no creature could hope to struggle free.

But Kadwyr's eye was quicker than the hunter's snare. With a taunting cackle the crow hopped into the air, flapped his wings, and flew from the branch to perch higher in the tree, where he peered down and brazenly waggled his tail feathers.

Leaving his net, with a snarl of anger the hunter unslung his bow, fitted an arrow to the string, and sent the shaft hissing straight for the crow.

Chuckling, Kadwyr fluttered his wings and sailed out of the path of the speeding arrow; then turned back to dance in the air in front of the furious hunter, who drew the bow again and again. Swooping and soaring, the crow dodged every shaft.

Seeing the hunter's quiver almost empty, Kadwyr grew even bolder, gliding closer, circling beyond reach, then swooping back to liven the game again. Gnashing his teeth at the elusive prey, the hunter struck out wildly, trying to seize the nimble crow.

Kadwyr sped away. As he flew, he turned his head in a backward glance to jeer at his defeated pursuer. In that heedless instant, the crow collided with a tree trunk.

Stunned, Kadwyr plummeted to the ground. The hunter ran toward him. Kadwyr croaked in pain as he strove to fly to safety. But his wing hung useless at his side, broken.

Breathless, Kadwyr scrambled into the bushes. The hunter plunged after him. Earthbound and wounded, Kadwyr began wishing he had not been so quick to turn down shelter from the squirrels and beavers. With the hunter gaining on him, the crow gladly would have squeezed into any tunnel, or burrow, or rabbit hole he could find. But all had been sealed, blocked, and barred with stones and twigs.

Dragging his wing, the crow skittered through the underbrush. His spindly legs were ill-suited to running, and he longed for the swiftness of the hare. He stumbled and went sprawling. An arrow buried itself in the ground beside him.

The hunter drew his bow. Though this was his pursuer's last arrow, Kadwyr knew himself a helpless target. Only a few paces away, the hunter took aim.

That same instant, a cloud of dust came whirling through the trees. Expecting in another moment to be skewered, Kadwyr now saw the hunter fling up his arms and drop his bow. The arrow clattered harmlessly into the leaves. Next, Kadwyr was sure his opponent had lost his wits. Roaring with pain, the hunter waved his arms and beat his hands against his face, trying to fend off the cloud buzzing about his head and shoulders.

The host of gnats swarmed over the raging hunter, darted into his ears and eyes, streamed up his nose and out his mouth. The more the hunter swept away the tiny creatures, the more they set upon him.

"Gwybeddin!" burst out the crow as one of the swarm broke from the cloud and lit on his beak. "Thank you for my life! Did I call you a flyspeck? You and your gnats are brave as eagles!"

"Hurry!" piped the gnat. "We're doing all we can, but he's more than a match for us. Quick, away with you!"

Kadwyr needed no urging. The gnats had saved him from

the hunter's arrows and, as well, had let him snatch a moment's rest. The crow set off again as fast as he could scramble through the dry leaves and dead branches of the forest floor.

Brave though Gwybeddin and his fellows had been, their efforts did not keep the hunter long from the chase. Soon Kadwyr head footfalls crashing close behind him. The hunter had easily found the crow's trail and seemed to gain in strength while his prey weakened with each step.

The crow plunged deeper into the woods, hoping to hide in a heavy growth of brambles or a thicket where the hunter could not follow. Instead, to Kadwyr's dismay, the forest here grew sparser. Before the crow could find cover, the hunter sighted him and gave a triumphant shout.

Not daring another backward glance, Kadwyr scrambled through a grove of trees. The ground before him lay clear and hard-packed; but while the way was easier for him, he realized it was easier, too, for his enemy to overtake him.

Just then Kadwyr heard a bellow of rage. The crow halted to see the hunter twisting and turning, struggling as if caught in his own net. Kadwyr stared in amazement. Amid the trees, Nedir and all the spiders in the forest had joined to spin their strongest webs. The strands were so fine the hunter had not seen them, but now they clung to him, twined and wrapped around him, and the more he tried to fight loose, the more they enshrouded him.

From a branch above Kadwyr's head, sliding down a single invisible thread, came Nedir, waving her long legs.

"We spinners and weavers have done our best," she called out, "but even our stoutest webs will soon give way. Be off, while you have the chance!"

"Granny Spider," cried the grateful Kadwyr, "forgive me if I ever made sport of you. Your knitting saved my neck!"

Once again the crow scurried away, sure this time he had escaped for good and all. Despite the pain in his wing, his spirits rose and he began gleefully cackling at the sight of the hunter so enmeshed in a huge cocoon.

But Kadwyr soon snapped his beak shut. His eyes darted about in alarm, for his flight had brought him to the edge of a steep cliff.

He halted and fearfully drew back. Without the use of his wing he would have fallen like a stone and been dashed to pieces on the rocks below. However, before he could decide which way to turn, he saw the hunter racing toward him.

Free of the spiders' webs, more enraged than ever, and bent on making an end of the elusive crow, the hunter pulled his knife from his belt. With a shout of triumph, he sprang at the helpless Kadwyr.

The crow, certain his last moment had come, flapped his one good wing and thrust out his beak, bound that he would sell his life dearly.

But the hunter stumbled in mid-stride. His foot caught on a round stone that tripped him up and sent him plunging headlong over the cliff.

Kadwyr's terror turned to joyous relief. He cawed, cackled, and crowed as loudly as any rooster. Then his beak fell open in astonishment.

The stone that had saved his life began to sprout four stubby legs and a tail; a leathery neck stretched out cautiously, and Crugan-Crawgan, the turtle, blinked at Kadwyr.

"Are you all right?" asked Crugan-Crawgan. "That is, I

mean to say . . . you've come to no harm? I'm sorry . . . ah, Kadwyr, there wasn't more I could have . . . done. We turtles, alas, can't run . . . like rabbits. Or fly . . . like eagles. But we are, I hope you'll agree . . . yes, we are solid, if nothing else. And . . . very, very steady."

"Crugan-Crawgan," said Kadwyr, "you saved my life and I thank you. Steady and solid you are, old fellow, and I'm glad of it."

"By the way," the turtle went on, "as I was saying . . . the last time we met. . . . Yes, the snail and I did have a race. It was . . . a draw."

The forest was again safe and the rejoicing animals came out of their hiding places. Edyrnion the eagle bore the wounded crow to Medwyn's valley, to be cared for and sheltered until his wing healed.

"Ah, Kadwyr, you scamp, I didn't expect to see you here so soon," Medwyn told the crow, who admitted all that had happened in the woods. "Your wing will mend and you'll be ready for some new scrape. But let us hope next time you can help your friends as they helped you."

"I know better than to scorn a spider," said Kadwyr, crestfallen. "I'll never taunt a turtle. And never again annoy a gnat. But — but, come to think of it," he went on, his eyes brightening, "if it hadn't been for me — yes, it was I! I who led that hunter a merry chase! I who saved all in the forest!"

Kadwyr chuckled and clucked, bobbed his head, and snapped his beak, altogether delighted with himself.

"Perhaps you did, at that," Medwyn gently answered. "In any case, go in peace, Kadwyr. The world has room enough for a rascal crow."

Caleb Thorne's Day

Elizabeth Coatsworth

The day was warm and a heat mirage hung over the waters of the Sound. The houses of Rhodanthe seemed to stand out of the sea, bare outlines of houses supported on nothing but their own reflections. Jim Midgett, sitting at the bow of his grandfather's fishing boat, half leaning against a coil of rope, was used to the sight, but it always gave him the feeling of being in a dream. His grandfather and his own younger brother Jo, aft in the cockpit, were silent. He could hear the flapping of fish against the boards, a little creaking of ropes, and the sigh of the water along their slowly moving keel. That was all. Behind them, thirty-five miles away, lay the low shore of Carolina, hidden far beyond sight. In front of them lay the great Atlantic and, apparently rising from the waves, this group of squares and oblongs that meant home, cutting the huge, lonely horizon of the sky. Nowhere was there the smallest glimpse of land.

"Reckon the Sound's covered the Banks again, Jo," said Jim.

"Reckon you're crazy," said Jo.

"Reckon the Sound *can* cover the Banks, can't it, grand-dad?" argued Jim.

"Reckon it can, Jim," said his grandfather, "but it's a long string of years since it did. I was about Jo's age here when it happened last, and I'll never forget it, if I live to be a hundred. Terrible wind from the southwest piled up the Sound water till it came over like a wall, clear to the sea. All heaving water as far as the eye could make out, with wreckage and chicken coops and the poor critters tossing about. Carried off the kitchen just after mother had put some ham on the stove to fry. She was laying the table, I recollect, and there was a crack to split your head, and the whole ell ripped off. Father cussed about that ham, more to keep up mother's spirits than anything else, I reckon. We none of us knew if the house wouldn't go next, but it held. Mother never was the same after that. When the waters parted again and the Banks showed up, same as ever, the rest of us went about our business, but mother kept the doors and windows shut ever after. Couldn't bear the sound of the waves on the beach, she said."

"Reckon she wasn't a real Banker," remarked Jo, a little scornfully.

"Yes, she was, too," answered his grandfather, sharply. "Born between tide and tide like the rest of us. But it's harder on the women. They don't get out in the boats as we do."

Old Captain Midgett grew silent, and Jim went on with his thoughts.

Yes, he thought to himself, it was a fine thing to be a Banker. Why, their family had been on the Banks ever since Sir Walter Raleigh's lost colony came there from Roanoke to get away from the Indians. Twenty miles of shore, past the bend of

Hatteras, what more could a man need to stretch his legs? And then there were always the boats. But the women stayed at home all day long, and the sand covered their little gardens and drifted under the sills of the doors. He remembered his mother saying once that she treasured the rooster more than a brooch of gold. "Something to listen to other than those screeching gulls," she had said. He secretly decided to bring her back a posy in a pot next time he went to Roanoke. He even pitied his younger sister Joanna a little, until he saw her standing on the shore in a faded red dress, skipping stones.

"Wake up, Jim! Wake up!" she cried, in her shrill little voice. "Pitch me the painter, Jim, quick!"

Jo, nearly a head shorter than Jim, was already nimbly over the side, wading to join her. Jim tumbled after him, his face reddening at being caught daydreaming again.

"Never you mind, Jim," said old Captain Midgett. "Reckon you got things going on inside your head that those young ones don't know anything about."

As they came up the steps, the old cock crowed; Ginger, the cat, rose slowly, arched her back, stretched each hind leg, and came forward at her own pace to be petted; while Spot, the hound, thumped the porch with his tail until it resounded like a drum.

Young Captain Midgett, the children's father, appeared from indoors, filling the doorway with his bulk.

"Hello, dad," he said. "Good fishing?"

"Nothing to complain of," answered old Captain Midgett.

"Had a good catch, myself," said young Captain Midgett. "Reckon we'll take the pink [a small, light fishing vessel] up to Norfolk. They say there's a good market right now up there."

Joanna whistled. Usually her father and the other men waited for the buyers, or occasionally went to Roanoke. Norfolk was quite another matter. They would be gone four or five days at least.

"Take me, too, dad?" she cried, swinging on his hand.

"What should I be doing with a big girl like you?" he asked. "You stay and help your mother."

"I could do a lot on the pink," said Jim, "and run errands in Norfolk."

"So could I," said Jo, not to be behind.

"Both of you stay right here, looking after things, while granddad and I are away," said young Captain Midgett, with a glance that warned them he would have no argument. "After supper I want you to take a letter for me to Captain Prudden about an errand I'm to do for him in the city."

That meant riding, for the captain lived four miles or more away in the next neighborhood. First the boys had to catch their ponies, which were grazing with the rest of the town horses and cows on the coarse beach grass. The little animals let themselves be caught and bridled easily enough, and trotted off side by side, with the boys on their backs, over the sand which would have brought an ordinary horse to a walk. But the Banks ponies were as used to the sand as the Bankers were, and had been there even longer. Their ancestors had been put ashore centuries before by the Spanish explorers in order to raise a supply of horses for their expeditions on the mainland.

It was getting dusk, and where the going was good the boys cantered the ponies. At one piece of broken wreckage on the beach, both animals shied violently. When they were by, Jim called to his brother, "Reckon it was a ghost they saw, Jo?"

"Reckon not," Jo called back, in his matter-of-fact way. "Horse will shy at most anything."

"Mighty lot of ghosts of drowned sailors along the beach, Jo," Jim argued.

"Didn't see nary ghost," said Jo.

"Horse can see a ghost before ever a man can," said Jim, and became silent. Looking over his shoulder, he saw that Spot, who was following them, avoided the wreckage, too; but there was no use arguing with a boy like Jo.

They were among the dead oaks now, great trees, whitened as driftwood, but standing upright in the sand, their broken stumps of branches jagged against the evening sky. A cow with a white face and long, twisted horns rose from a dune and gave them a wild, mournful stare.

"Reckon this is where they used to hang the pirates, Jo," said Jim.

"They always hung pirates on the mainland, and you know it," said Jo, somewhat annoyed at Jim's gloomy conversation.

"Then reckon this is where the pirates used to hang other folks. Granddad says Blackbeard used to be hereabouts, with his long black beard combed and braided into two braids and their ends looped up over his ears. You've heard of Blackbeard, Jo?"

"Can't you talk of anything except ghosts and Blackbeards at this time of the night, Jim Midgett?" demanded Jo angrily, switching his pony into a canter to stop all possibility of further conversation.

They made good time to Captain Prudden's, and reached his doorstep just as Mrs. Prudden was lighting the lamp in the kitchen.

It seemed to both boys that Captain Prudden took a long

time to find his glasses and read their father's letter, and then an even longer time to get out ink and paper and to write a slow reply. By the time that Jim, as the oldest, had the letter safely in his pocket, it was nearly dark, and the waves gleamed a dim white among the resounding beaches. This time it was Jo who walked wide of the Prudden graves by the front fence as they unhitched their ponies.

"Oh, *they* don't walk," Jim reassured him. "They're at home. It's those on the beaches that no one ever found."

The night was full of sounds and the vague movement of water. A sleeping seal woke and flopped awkwardly down the dark beach. The ponies snorted and threw up their heads. A piece of driftwood, ending in a knot of whitened roots, for a moment seemed to reach toward them like a skeleton hand. Both the ponies and their riders were out of breath by the time they drew down to a walk in the shelter of the scattered lights of Rhodanthe.

The next day the pink sailed, and Jim and Jo and Joanna and Spot were all down on the shore to see it off. Just before he left, young Captain Midgett put his hand for a moment on Jim's shoulder.

"You're the oldest, Jim," he said. "You're in charge."

"Just keep off the water on Caleb Thorne's day, and I reckon you young ones can take care of yourselves," said old Captain Midgett.

With the men of the family gone, the children were on their best behavior. Joanna's curly head could be seen at the kitchen window, where she stood washing dishes instead of vanishing like quicksilver the moment the last spoon was laid down and the last mouthful eaten. The boys took the small boat fishing on Pamlico Sound, but for the first two days their luck was bad. They had been particularly anxious to make a good showing while their father was away.

The third day was Caleb Thorne's day, a fine blue day with just enough wind for good sailing.

"Reckon we'll mend nets today," said Jim at breakfast, regretfully, eating his tenth pancake.

"Whyever can't we go fishing just because of old Caleb Thorne?" asked Jo, rebelliously kicking at the leg of the table.

"Just stop that, Jo Midgett," said his mother. "No one goes fishing on Caleb Thorne's day, and you know it."

"If no one ever does, how does anyone know they'd get drowned if they did?" asked Joanna, who loved to argue.

"Because people *have* gone and they *have* been drowned," said Mrs. Midgett firmly.

"Well, but who, mother?" said Jo. "Who? I dare you to say who."

"There was a man named Will Elwell when I was a girl," replied Mrs. Midgett somberly. "He went out on Caleb Thorne's day. It was a fine day like today, and it stayed fine and stayed fine. Everyone began to say, 'Reckon maybe Will Elwell's right.' Then along about four o'clock there came a burst of wind out of nowhere. Didn't blow more than five minutes, but no one ever saw Will Elwell again."

Mrs. Midgett's story was followed by silence. Even Jo and Joanna were convinced for the time at least. But sitting on the warm sand, the big net across their knees, the light wind blowing by them, Joanna returned to the discussion in a roundabout way.

"Reckon lots of people been drowned who weren't fishing on Caleb Thorne's day and never had nary glimpse of Caleb Thorne."

"Reckon," said Jim, working steadily.

There was a long silence while three sea gulls winged their way overhead, crossing from the Sound to the sea.

"Reckon lots of people fish on Caleb Thorne's day and don't get drowned," went on Joanna in a low voice.

"Reckon they *don't*, Joanna," said Jim, looking up. "Didn't you hear what mother said?"

"That was only one man, and it might have happened anyway," said Jo, coming into the discussion.

"It mightn't," said Jim.

"It might, too," said Jo and Joanna together.

"Happens every time," said Jim.

"Who else ever got drowned?" asked Jo.

"Lots," said Jim.

"Name them!" cried Joanna, triumphantly.

"I can't, but I know it's true. None of the men go out," replied Jim staunchly.

Joanna again returned to the attack from a different angle. "If Will Elwell got drowned, who knows he saw Caleb Thorne's boat?"

"They know right enough."

"How do they know, Jim Midgett?"

"Because they do, that's all."

They all went on mending the net for a while longer. It was Jo who broke the silence.

"I don't believe there ever was any Caleb Thorne, anyhow, and if there was, I don't believe he ever said, 'I'll finish my catch

if I have to fish till judgment day'; and if he did, I don't believe
he disappeared in a gale of wind; and if he did disappear, I don't
believe that he still fishes every year on that day and that if anyone sees him they'll be drowned too, so there! It's just as
Joanna says. If they're drowned, how can they tell they've seen
Caleb Thorne fishing? It's just a story some one made up, and
everyone's scared for fear it *might* be true."

"You think you know everything, Jo Midgett," said Jim.
"You think you know more than dad and granddad and all the
Bankers put together. It's only one person *has* to be drowned,
I reckon. Maybe some of them get back to shore and tell."

By this time Jo and Joanna were in open rebellion. Eyes
shining with excitement, they had dropped work on the net.
They exchanged glances.

"Reckon I'll go fishing," said Jo, in what he hoped was his
everyday voice.

"Reckon I'll come with you," said Joanna. "Must have fish
to show dad when he gets back."

"Reckon you won't, either of you!" said Jim. "You heard
what granddad said. Why, even father doesn't go out on Caleb
Thorne's day, and he isn't afraid of anything on land or sea.
You can't go, I say!"

"Who's going to stop us, then?" asked Jo, getting up and
squaring off. He was shorter and younger than Jim, but he was
more heavily built, and the boys were nearly an even match.

"Mother'll stop you."

"Tattletale, tattletale," shrieked Jo and Joanna.

No, Jim must see it through himself. Helplessly he followed
the other two down to the shore and watched them make ready.
Not a soul was in sight. Spot stood wagging his tail hopefully.

He didn't care with whom he went, so long as he could go sailing. As the children pushed off, he jumped over the side and landed in the cockpit, with a great scraping of claws. Joanna was already in, pulling up the sail. Jo was scrambling in after her.

The blackness of despair closed over Jim. His father had left him in charge. How could he ever face him and tell him that the other children had been lost on Caleb Thorne's day? Quickly he waded after the boat and, just as it steadied to the breeze, pulled himself over the stern.

Jo grinned impishly. "Hello," he said, "who's here?"

Jim grinned back. He was in for whatever was to happen. The decision had been taken out of his hands. Now matters were up to Caleb Thorne.

All day long not a cloud crossed the sky, and there was only enough breeze for sailing. The fishing was better than any they had ever known.

"Won't dad be surprised?" Joanna kept asking excitedly. "Aren't the others foolish to stay ashore when they could be getting a catch like this?"

Fishing was in their blood. And soon they had almost forgotten that this was a day with a curse on it, for, after all, they came of a people who lived always under the threat of danger. There were fresh water and biscuits stowed away under one of the seats, and when they were hungry they ate and drank quickly, begrudging every minute lost from their lines. Only Jim kept an anxious eye on the sky, an anxious ear intent on the quality of the wind. But hour followed hour, and sky and sea remained calm and clear. The boat rose and dipped quietly on an untroubled swell, while the cockpit grew heavier and heavier with its load of fish.

Old Spot rose, shook himself, and climbed to the decked-in space by the mast to get the last of the sun. The light had not grown less, but the breeze was cooler.

"Better be getting home," said Jim.

"Reckon we had," said Jo. After all, enough was enough of a good thing, and he, too, had heard about Caleb Thorne ever since he was born.

Only Joanna wanted to catch a few more.

"Just like a girl, never knowing when to quit," said Jo. Joanna stuck out her tongue at him, but drew in her line. Jim swung the boat toward Rhodanthe, which appeared more like a distant fleet of vessels on the horizon than the homes of human beings. The breeze which they had had all day held steady — a following breeze which every minute brought them nearer home. The houses of Rhodanthe grew larger; the beach appeared. They could even make out the distant boats pulled up on the shore.

Jim gave an unconscious sigh of relief. There was a whine from Spot and a sudden chill in the air.

"What's that astern?" asked Joanna in a whisper, pale with terror. Jim saw Jo's eyes look past him, fixed and staring, and swung his own head over his shoulder. A low fog had come in behind them and was moving down upon them with terrifying speed, rushing over the water, which was whipped into one long sheet of spray.

"A white squall," thought Jim, sitting paralyzed at the tiller.

A white squall, coming so suddenly out of perfect weather, was unearthly and horrible enough, but in the whiteness he thought he saw something whiter still, the shape of a sail, the outline of an onward-driven boat.

Jo was praying loudly. The outskirts of the wind had struck them, the water hissed about them.

"Take the tiller, Joanna!" Jim screamed, pushing the handle into her cold hand and stumbling forward to where Spot was crouched in the cockpit near the stern.

Images stabbed his mind: Dad, Caleb Thorne — Something had to be drowned. He caught the struggling hound, lifted him, and with a great effort succeeded in pushing him overboard. Then he let go the halyards, which brought down their single sail in a pile of fluttering canvas, and was back in time to catch the tiller as the squall struck them. All was whiteness about them and a shrieking of icy wind, and their boat tore ahead under its bare pole. Fast as they went, something passed by them faster still, something that looked like a small fishing vessel, almost lost to sight in the spray and fog. In a breathtakingly short time the squall had passed them and they were left drenched and shaken in a boat rocking crazily.

"We've seen Caleb Thorne," said Joanna, first to recover her power of speech.

"Poor old Spot," said Jo, beginning to cry. "I wouldn't have lost him for ten catches of fish! It's all my fault that Spot's drowned."

Jim was busy with the sail, so that they could get home as soon as possible. He could still feel Spot's weight in his arms, and his heart was heavier than Jo's.

"Spot isn't drowned," said Joanna in surprise. "Didn't you see Caleb Thorne pull him aboard? Reckon he wanted company, and Spot always was one to like sailing."

"I didn't see any such thing," said Jo. "Just something white a-driving by, lickety-cut."

"Reckon you were too scared to see," said Joanna with a touch of satisfaction. "Reckon my eyes are sharper than yours. Won't it make a tale on the Banks, though, us meeting with Caleb Thorne and bringing home our catch of fish, anyhow?"

The beach stretched before them. They saw people running toward them down the sand. Their mother was there, waving a red tablecloth, and around their feet were the fish floating about in a cockpit half-filled with water. All the rest seemed a sudden nightmare, come and gone like a clap of thunder. Even Joanna began to doubt her own senses.

"I did see Spot pulled aboard, Jim, didn't I?" asked Joanna beseechingly. All that had been so clear to her five minutes before now seemed hazy and uncertain.

"Reckon you did, Joanna," said Jim, reassuring her. "It did just tear me to do that, but if I hadn't, we'd *all* have been drowned together. As it was, the center of the squall never struck us. We just got the edge of it."

"And that was squall enough," said Jo. "Everything was white. I wonder, did we really see another boat?"

"As sure as we're alive this minute," said Jim stoutly. "And somehow I reckon we'll know for sure about Spot."

And Jim proved to be right. They never found Spot's body, but it was Jim who came across his old collar washed up on the shore. Caleb Thorne had let them know for sure that Spot was safe with him.

The Dancing Camel

Betsy Byars

On the hot, white desert moved a long line of camels. They walked slowly, surely, following one behind the other like a string of beads.

Suddenly the camel at the end of the line gave a graceful hop. She stepped to the side, paused, pointed her toe, turned around, pointed her toe again, bowed, and then followed the other camels.

No one in the caravan noticed what the last camel had done, and the camels moved on as before.

After a while it happened again. The last camel gave two hops, turned to the right, turned to the left, swayed back and forth, clapped her feet together, ended in a graceful bow, and then followed the other camels. No one in the caravan noticed what the last camel had done, and the camels moved on as before.

All across the desert, while the other camels moved slowly and evenly, the last camel, Camilla, was stepping and pointing and bowing and spinning and swaying.

Now it happened that a lone man on a camel was passing

the same way. He was known as Abul the Tricky, and he was making his way from the town which could be seen on the horizon. As he sat on his camel, he looked toward the caravan.

The camels moved slowly, surely, following one behind the other. Suddenly at the end of the line Camilla gave a light leap. She crossed her legs, pointed her toes, hopped backward and forward, bowed sedately, then followed the other camels.

No one in the caravan noticed what she had done, and the caravan moved on as before.

But Abul the Tricky had noticed. He passed his hand over his eyes. "Does the sun play tricks on me," he asked, sitting straighter on his camel, "or was that a *dancing* camel?"

He shielded his eyes from the sun and stared through the waving heat to the last camel. He urged his own camel closer.

"It could not be," he muttered. "Such a thing could not be."

Suddenly, as he watched, the last camel in the line paused. She stamped her right foot, stamped her left foot, tossed her head two times and then spun slowly around, falling finally into a graceful crouch. Then, with another toss of her head, she rose and followed the other camels.

"It is! A dancing camel!" he cried, pressing his camel into a run. "I have got to have her." He threw back his head and laughed in his delight. "Ah, there is no other camel in the world such as this. She will be famous. First she will dance in the market place, then in the Sultan's Palace, then all over the world. I MUST have that camel."

Without pausing, he rode to the front of the caravan and raised one hand in greeting to the leader.

When the leader of the caravan saw Abul the Tricky, he stopped and tapped his camel lightly. The camel knelt so he could dismount.

"I am Abul," said Abul the Tricky with a slight bow. "And you? You are the owner of these camels?"

"That is right," said the leader. "What is it you want?"

"I do not know if you are aware of this," Abul said, stepping closer, "but there is something wrong with the last camel in your caravan."

The caravan leader turned slowly to look at the end of the line where Camilla was spinning with one foot in the air.

"Camilla Camel? There is nothing wrong with her."

"But I saw her! While the other camels walk, she moves this way — she moves that way."

"Oh, yes, she moves this way, that way. She is a dancing camel."

"I should think she would not be a good worker," Abul the Tricky said with his eyes closing slightly.

"No, she is not a worker, but she is a pleasing animal."

"I tell you. I could use a camel such as that. She is no worker, as you agree, but I will take her off your hands."

"What would you do with such a camel?"

Abul shrugged. "Perhaps I would let her dance in the market place. Who knows?"

The caravan leader smiled. He shook his head. "You do not understand. Camilla only dances for her own enjoyment, because she is happy here with the caravan. The hot sands, the warm air, this is why she dances."

Abul the Tricky shook his head impatiently. "Sell her to me."

The caravan leader smiled again. "That is not a bad camel you have there. Let us trade. I will take your camel. You will take Camilla."

"Agreed," said Abul quickly, and while the little caravan paused there in the desert, the exchange was made.

"Come, Camilla," said Abul. He leaned close and put his hand on her neck. "Let us go to the city. There you will begin your life as a dancer. I will give you everything, EVERYTHING, and you will dance for me. That is fair, eh? You will dance and I will become the richest man in the world. How does that sound, my pretty?"

Camilla Camel looked out over the desert. She waited quietly until Abul was on her back, then she began to move toward the city. Suddenly she stopped. She stooped once, straightened, stooped twice, straightened, stooped a third time, and then straightened quickly and pointed her toes five times.

Abul the Tricky laughed, his teeth gleaming in the sun. "Ah, she is dancing!" he cried. "And she is mine, all mine!"

As Camilla and Abul the Tricky entered the city, two men who were standing in a nearby doorway came forward. One was fat, the other tall. The tall one spoke first. "Ah, it is Abul the Tricky returning to our city. What brings you to our gates again?"

"You will not believe this, my friends, but I am at this very moment riding the treasure of the desert!"

"I see only a camel," said the fat one, squinting in the sun.

"Not *only* a camel, my friend. This splendid beast is a DANCING camel."

The fat man and the tall man looked at each other and laughed. "Last time it was a magic bottle," said the tall one.

"We had only to give you a gold piece, rub the bottle, and all our wishes would come true."

The fat man stopped laughing. "I remember," he said darkly. "And before that it was a machine that made gold. Bah! Magic bottles! Gold machines! Dancing camels! You'll not trick us this time, Abul."

"But it is true, my friends. Look on this dainty creature. Is she not fair? Is she not graceful? Can you not recognize a dancing camel when you see one?"

"She looks no different from any other camel," said the tall man.

"Come to the market tonight. You will see her dance. Tell everyone!" He rode on with a wave of his hand. "Tell *everyone!*" He threw back his head and laughed. "Abul has a DANC-ING CAMEL!"

The word spread quickly throughout the city. Children stopped their play to speak with wide, dark eyes of the dancing camel; men laughed and talked of Camilla Camel over their coffee; women whispered of her behind their veils. Excitement rose. Soon everyone in the city knew that a camel was to dance in the market place that evening.

Only Camilla Camel stood calm in the midst of the bustle and excitement. She looked quietly out over the crowds who came to stare at her. She did not move when Abul placed a scarlet harness with brass bells about her neck. She stepped back only once when the three musicians Abul had hired came and practiced their music in her ear. Her eyes looked always over the wooden roofs of the shops to the long flowing desert beyond.

By evening, everyone in the city was pressing into the market place.

"Make room," Abul shouted. "Make room for everyone. I want everyone to see the dancing camel. There never has been such a thing in all the world. And it is here, here in our little town that she will dance first. Come, everyone!"

He did not need to urge. Everyone wanted to see the dancing camel, and they pressed forward eagerly. Camilla Camel stepped back two steps.

"Quiet, now quiet, please," Abul said with both hands lifted. "In a moment the camel will dance as I have promised, and then these small boys will pass among you and you will put coins in their trays."

A rumble of displeasure came from the crowd. "You said nothing of coins," one man called out.

"Anyone who does not want to see the dancing camel," Abul said, "may now leave the market place."

He waited. No one spoke. No one moved. No one left.

"Ah, how wise you are," Abul said. His teeth gleamed as he smiled. "Someday you will tell your grandchildren that you were in the market place the night Camilla Camel danced."

In the middle of the crowd Camilla Camel moved her feet uneasily, and the brass bells of her harness sounded in the evening air.

"Not yet! Not yet!" cried Abul. "Wait for the music. Now, you musicians. PLAY. Play as you have never played before. And, Camilla Camel, *dance*. DANCE!"

The three musicians lifted their instruments, and the low wail of their music filled the air. So beautifully did they play that some of the people began to sway and pat their hands together. Abul moved in front of Camilla Camel and patted his hands.

"Dance," he said. "Dance, O Beauty of the Desert. Dance! Dance as you danced in the desert. Bow, nod, turn, DANCE!"

Camilla Camel stood quietly in the midst of the crowd. She did not move at all. She did not even look at Abul patting his hands before her. Her eyes looked ever toward the horizon.

"Dance, Camilla, dance." Abul reached down and touched one of her feet. "*Dance!* Don't you remember?" He tried to lift one of her feet and kick it in the air. "Remember?" He shook her harness so that the bells rang gaily.

Camilla moved her feet closer together and was still.

"Dance, Camilla," said Abul. He began some lively steps of his own to show her what he meant. "See, Camilla! DANCE."

But Camilla looked above him and did not move at all.

"Ah, is this another of your tricks, Abul?" one of the crowd called.

"Yes, where is the dancing camel? We look and look but we see only an ordinary beast."

"Wait, wait," cried Abul. "She will dance. Only give her a moment. Come, Camilla, dance." He turned to the musicians. "Can you play no better? Give her a lively tune, a gay tune. Then she will dance."

The musicians stopped and after a brief conference began such a lively tune that more of the people began to clap and sway in time.

"Now she will dance," Abul said. "Come, Camilla, now you *must* dance. The crowd grows restless. Come, dance."

Camilla Camel did not move. In the midst of the shifting, swaying crowd she stood like an unyielding palm tree.

"Bah! It is only another of Abul's tricks! Let us leave!" one man said in disgust and, turning his back, walked away.

"It is no trick, I tell you. This *is* a dancing camel. Listen, listen, perhaps she is tired — yes, that is the trouble. Tonight she will rest, and tomorrow she will dance. Come tomorrow. Everyone come tomorrow."

The musicians ceased playing, the people began to leave the market place, and the boys who were to pass among the people collecting coins put down their trays.

"Tomorrow morning!" shouted Abul at their backs. "Everyone return in the morning."

But the next morning the market place was only half filled. Abul was not dismayed. "You can be glad you came, my friends," he told the small crowd gathered there. "You can tell the others that you saw Camilla Camel dance in the market place."

"We had better see Camilla dance in the market place, or we leave," said one man.

"She will dance," Abul said. "Come, Camilla, it is time. You have slept on the finest straw, you have eaten the finest food, you wear the loveliest harness. Now you must dance for me." He waved his hands, and the musicians began to play.

"Dance, Camilla, please, dance. Just one simple step," he pleaded.

Camilla shifted her weight once and then stood still.

"Again he tricks us! Come, we waste no more time here." And before Abul could stop them, the people began to depart. Soon Abul and Camilla Camel stood alone.

Abul sat down and bowed his head. "She will not dance. She will not dance," he muttered. "I am ruined. My money is gone. I have nothing left but a camel who will not dance."

Suddenly a shadow fell across Abul's bowed head. He looked up to see the caravan leader standing before him.

"What is wrong, my friend?" he asked Abul.

"What is wrong! Did you not see? I have a dancing camel who will not dance. That is what is wrong."

The caravan leader smiled. "It was not to be. Camilla can not dance here where she is not happy."

"It is easy for you to smile, my friend," said Abul with a frown. "You do not own a stubborn camel who will not dance."

"That is so. I no longer own the camel. And I find, now that I am ready to take my small caravan back across the desert, that I miss Camilla Camel."

"Miss this beast? This stone of the desert?" Suddenly Abul stopped. "You miss this camel?" he asked quietly.

The caravan leader nodded.

Abul got slowly to his feet. His teeth gleamed suddenly in the morning sun. "I tell you," he said. "Of course I want to keep this camel — a dancing camel is a rare animal. But I understand that you want her. I will trade her back to you."

"I will give you your camel in return," said the caravan leader.

Abul hesitated. "But, you see, I have spent much money on this camel. I have bought her this fine harness, food, and straw." He stopped abruptly. "That is a handsome ring you are wearing, my friend."

The caravan leader held up his hand to show a large silver ring set with a white stone.

"An uncle of mine, a man of great wealth, had such a ring," Abul said. "He told me it was a ring of good fortune."

The caravan leader smiled and shook his head. "This is no ring of good fortune," he said. "It is an ordinary ring I bought in the market place."

Abul's eyes gleamed as he bent over the ring. "Give it to me and the camel is yours."

"But this is not a ring of good fortune," the caravan leader protested.

"I must have it," said Abul, stepping forward in his eagerness.

With a shrug the caravan leader twisted the ring from his finger and handed it to Abul. Then he led Camilla away. She went eagerly, her head lifted to catch sight of the small caravan loading just outside the city.

Abul the Tricky barely noticed their departure.

"See what I have!" he cried. "Come, everyone, look."

"What now? How do you trick us this time?" said a man leaning in the doorway of his café.

"No trick, it is no trick. I have a ring of good fortune. Whoever wears this ring has good fortune. See, I have worn the ring only a moment and already I feel my fortune has changed. Who would wear the ring next?"

"I, Abul," said the man. He left the doorway of his shop. "I am in need of good fortune. I have no business. No one comes to drink my coffee."

Abul stepped closer to the man. "For one coin, one small coin," he whispered, "you may wear the ring."

The man drew back at the mention of the coin. "I do not know," he said.

"Very well," said Abul. "I will give another the chance to wear the ring."

"No, no, I will wear the ring. Give it to me." The man took the ring and gave a coin to Abul.

Slowly, one by one, people began to return to the market place. One by one, they entered the café to see the ring of good fortune.

"See," cried Abul in great spirits. "He wears the ring of good fortune only a moment, and already his shop is filled with customers. Come and see, everyone."

"But, Abul," protested the man, "Abul, my shop is filled, but no one buys my coffee. Abul, hear me, hear me."

Around the café crowded the people. "Abul has a ring of good fortune," they said excitedly.

"Who would wear the ring next?" shouted Abul above the noise.

"I, Abul, I."

"No, I."

Just outside the city, while the people gathered at the café, Camilla Camel was led to the caravan. She took her place at the end of the line. She stood quietly while the caravan leader mounted his camel and rode to the front.

Across the hot, white desert, the long line of camels began to move. They walked slowly, surely, following one behind the other like a string of beads.

Suddenly at the end of the line, Camilla gave a high joyous leap. She pointed her toes, dipped to the right, dipped to the left, touched her toes together, spun around three times, and fell in a graceful kneel. Then she got up and followed the other camels.

No one in the caravan noticed what Camilla had done, and the camels moved on as before.

The Library Book

Lois Lenski

"Mr. Bonehead was just a dummy, made of wood," said the boys.

"He walked and he talked!" said the girls.

There was great excitement at recess. A woman and a man had brought a ventriloquist act to school, and all the children were talking about it.

"That lady, Madame Simonds, made him walk by winding up something in the back," said Jolene Burgess.

"She made him talk by moving her own lips, only you couldn't see her do it," added Shirley Mason.

"Oh, I've heard lots of that stuff over the radio," said one of the boys.

"But it's better to see it — a wooden dummy talking," said Bug Burgess.

"He sure did look real," said Joanda.

"How could he cry when he was made of wood?" asked Ricky. He was out of his cast now and back at school again.

"Likely she had a rubber ball with water in it," said Shirley, "and she squirted it."

The children laughed.

"But how did he know everybody's names?" asked Joanda.

"Oh, Steve told her when he helped her unload her truck this morning," said Mavis. "I saw him pointing out different kids to her."

"Look! Here they come!"

The children ran to the door and Madame Simonds came down the steps with her bags and props, and a long roll of stage scenery. The boys ran to help her. Then came her helper, little Mr. Whoozit, carrying the dummy slung over his shoulder. Joanda got a close look at Mr. Bonehead. His eyes and mouth were painted in bright colors on his carved face. He wore a red hat with a long feather, and had on a Mexican coat with sparklers over it. The children reached up to touch the sparklers.

"Are you afraid of him?" Joanda asked Ricky.

"Course not." Ricky poked the dummy's eyes with his fingers. "He don't even wink."

They watched as the man and woman packed their belongings into their car. It had a Texas license.

"Gee! That was the best show I ever saw!" said Ricky. He turned to Joanda, but she had already gone inside.

In the schoolhouse, the hall was empty and quiet.

Joanda went to the bubbler and for the first time took a drink of water from it. It was better than drinking out of a dipper. She walked down the hall. Quietly she pushed open the swinging door of the new dining room. She had never been inside. No one was there. Mrs. Bronson, the cook, must have stepped out for a minute. So Joanda went in on tiptoe.

There were two long low tables and two higher ones, covered with pretty oil cloth. They had bouquets of flowers in the middle. There were red-checked curtains at the windows and green ferns on the window sills. Big pots of food were simmering on the stove, and the smell was delicious. Joanda wished that she and her brothers and sister could eat there.

Near the stove was a sink, and one of the taps was running. Joanda tiptoed over to turn it off. Then she stopped just in time. She nearly fell over with surprise. Stuffing both hands over her mouth, she caught herself before she made a sound.

There was Miss Fenton down on her hands and knees under the sink, putting something into a paper sack. She was so busy she did not look up. Joanda stared. She saw what Miss Fenton was picking up. She tiptoed back out as quickly and quietly as she could. She was sure Miss Fenton had not seen her.

After the entertainers drove off, the children settled down to Arithmetic, and then the bell rang for lunch. Joanda thought unhappily of her cold lunch. It was "fried pies" again — she had seen Mama fixing them. She never liked them much. They always made her stomach ache all afternoon, they were so heavy. They were made of left-over biscuit dough, cut in circles by a saucer, then folded over with a few dried, stewed peaches inside, and fried in deep fat. She thought with longing of the appetizing smell in the school dining room.

The hot lunch children filed down the hall, where Mrs. Bronson was soon heaping their plates high. The cold lunch children huddled around the little table in the back of Miss Fenton's room, where their lunches were piled.

Miss Fenton came in hurriedly and seemed excited. She picked up one lunch wrapped in a transparent bread paper. "Whose is this?" she asked. A pale-faced boy called Glenwood claimed it. Miss Fenton opened the paper.

"Why, it's got cockroaches in it!" she exclaimed.

The children jumped back.

"Don't put one on me!" cried Ricky.

Miss Fenton opened a lunch wrapped in newspaper, another in a sugar sack, and finally Joanda's paper sack.

"Why, they've all got cockroaches in them," she said. "They're not fit to eat. You'll have to come into the dining room and eat hot lunches today."

She looked at Joanda. "Is Ricky's in the same sack with yours?"

"Yes ma'am," said Joanda, dropping her eyes.

"I wonder how the cockroaches got in here," said Miss Fenton. "We've had plenty in the kitchen. We must buy some roach powder."

It was very funny. Joanda was afraid to look Miss Fenton straight in the eyes for fear she would laugh. Then she knew she must not give Miss Fenton away, for she understood *why* she had done it. Suddenly she was very happy. At last they could eat with the other children.

"COCKROACHES IN THE COLD LUNCHES THIS MORNING!" announced Miss Fenton in a loud voice, as she led the children in.

They were greeted by a chorus of laughter, but a table was ready, so they sat down. Joanda and Ricky were hungry. They each ate two platefuls and they drank all their milk. Miss Fenton was pleased, but what would Mama say?

Still stranger things happened that afternoon. Miss Fenton was an unusual teacher. She was always surprising the children by doing things never done in school before. In Fourth Grade spelling, she asked, "Who knows what *permanent* means?" The children could spell it, but did not know its meaning.

Joanda held up her hand. "It means something that lasts forever."

Miss Fenton was pleased and asked Joanda how she knew.

"I read it in the newspaper." She did not add that the newspaper was pasted upside-down on the wall.

The children used the word in sentences. They talked of *permanent friendships* — friends you know all your life; and of *permanent homes.*

"Do you mean the kind you never move away from?" asked Joanda.

Miss Fenton said yes. Then she mentioned *permanents,* the kind of curl that stays in your hair.

"My Mama's gonna git one next fall," said Joanda, "if we make a good cotton crop."

The children laughed and made Joanda feel ashamed. She wished she hadn't said it.

The rest of the afternoon was given to a Beauty Parlor and Barber Shop party. When the lunch dishes were washed, Mrs. Bronson came in to help. The school nurse arrived in her car, bringing the equipment.

Everybody's hair was to be washed. The nurse used coal oil on some of the heads first, then a sweet-smelling shampoo. Mrs. Bronson was the barber and with her electric clippers soon had the shaggy heads of the boys looking like shorn sheep.

It was fun, and all the children laughed. "Cut mine! Cut mine!" they begged.

Joanda sat on the bench, with Ricky by her side, her hand clutching his tightly, waiting with the others. Because everybody else was doing it, they'd have to do it too. At last their turn came. Mrs. Bronson snipped Ricky and the nurse shampooed Joanda. Then Miss Fenton took a pair of shears and began to cut her hair.

"Oh, *don't!*" Joanda screamed and jumped from her chair. "You just better not cut my hair, you old teacher, you!" she cried. "My mother didn't say you could do it." Anger changed her pretty face to an ugly one. "I saw what you did! I saw you put those cockroaches in our paper sack! *I saw you!*"

Miss Fenton's face turned red. Fortunately most of the children had already left the room. She ignored the girl's remark completely. She had the nurse explain to Joanda how much easier it is to take proper care of the hair when it is short. Miss Fenton had asked all the mothers' permissions except Joanda's, because Joanda had been absent the day before.

"Since you feel the way you do, I'll just trim off the ends a little." Reluctantly, Joanda sat down. "I'll trim it off even and then put it up in curlers. I have a pretty silk scarf for you to tie over your head, Joanda. You leave the curlers on until tomorrow morning, and you'll be surprised how pretty your hair will be — as pretty as a real permanent."

Joanda frowned and did not answer. As she sat there she grew more and more worried. Mama would see that hers and Ricky's hair had been cut and Ricky would tell about the hot lunch. Mama would be mad as hops.

That afternoon, Joanda was afraid to go in the house when she got home from school. She cut across the cotton field with Jolene Burgess and went up to their house and played till dark.

Then she came home, opened the front door softly and crept in. Mama was busy getting supper in the kitchen. Mavis and Steve were talking about the ventriloquist show and Ricky was trying to talk like Mr. Bonehead. He must have forgotten to mention the hot lunch and the barber shop. But why didn't Mama notice his hair had been cut?

Joanda took her clothes off quietly and slipped into bed. She covered her head with the quilt. The silk scarf was a pretty one, bright blue with yellow lilies on it. But Mama mustn't see it. The curlers hurt her head, but she couldn't help it. She must leave them on till morning as Miss Fenton had told her to do.

Ricky came in the bedroom, and seeing a bump in the bed, punched her.

"Stop it!" she said.

"Nannie's in bed, Mama," said Ricky. "Nannie's gone to bed without her supper."

"What's the matter?" called Mama. "Don't you feel good?"

"Got the stomach ache," said Joanda. She remembered the stomach ache she would have had if she'd eaten the fried pies for lunch.

"Want some castor oil?" called Daddy.

"No, it's not that bad," answered Joanda.

The family laughed.

"Comin' out to supper, Nannie?" called Steve, a little later.

"No, I'm not hungry. Just sleepy."

They let her alone after that. She fell asleep to the murmur of their voices.

Joanda woke up early the next morning. Mama was in the kitchen and had started the fire. Lolly was walking around, climbing up on things and talking. Lolly could say many words now.

Joanda heard the singing of the teakettle and the clatter of the dishes. She smelled the appetizing odors of boiling coffee and sizzling grease. She heard Mama open the oven door to put the biscuits in. Breakfast would soon be ready.

"Git up, you lazy bones!" called Mama.

Joanda heard Lolly say, "I wanna big biscuit with grease gravy and syrup on it. Mama, is the gravy done?"

"It's on the table, now leave it alone like a good girl," said Mama.

Joanda came to the kitchen door as soon as she was dressed and stood watching sleepily. "Lolly," she said, "who likes you best?"

"You do, Nannie," said the little girl.

"Lolly, who's mean to you?" asked Joanda.

"Ever'body's mean to me 'ceptin' Nannie!"

A bucket of water with a dipper in it sat on a chair. Lolly put one foot on the rung of this chair, then stepped with her other foot onto her own chair.

"I'm hungry," she said. "I want gravy quick."

Her foot slipped. As she threw her hand up, she knocked the bowl of hot gravy and spilled it over her hand and arm. She screamed loudly.

Joanda got to her first and pulled her away from the table. Mama ran over and wiped the gravy off with a dish towel.

"She's burned," said Mama. "Git some coal oil quick."

Joanda's hands shook so she could hardly tip the can and pour it. She brought a saucerful to Mama, who dipped the towel and wrapped it around the baby's arm as quickly as she could. All this time Lolly was screaming.

Daddy and the other children had jumped into their clothes and stood looking. "I'll take her to the doctor," Daddy said.

Mama said, "All right, let's go." She started to take Lolly

from Joanda's arms, but couldn't. Lolly clung tightly to her sister, crying hard.

"You'll have to go along, Nannie," said Daddy.

"Can't we go too?" asked the other children. "You can drop us off at school on the way back."

"Well, get in," said Daddy.

Mama took the biscuits out of the oven and let them sit to turn cold. Breakfast was forgotten as they climbed into the truck. Joanda and Lolly rode with Mama and Daddy in front, and the others in the back. Lolly had quieted down and seemed to be sleeping on Joanda's shoulder.

"Will any doctor be up this early?" asked Mama.

"Which one will we go to?" asked Daddy

"I don't know," said Mama. "Got any money in your pocket?"

"About fifty cents," said Daddy. "Let's go to a drug store first and ask what's good for a burn. Likely we could git something for fifty cents."

"We'll let the druggist look at it," said Mama, "and if he says she needs a doctor, we'll ask him which one to go to."

Joanda held Lolly while the druggist unwrapped her arm. He said the burn was not serious. He covered the baby's arm with salve and bandaged it. He gave Mama a tube of the salve for fifty cents. Lolly began to talk and laugh on the way home, so they knew she was all right.

Mama didn't notice Joanda's hair until they stopped by the schoolhouse to let the children off.

"What you done to your hair, Nannie?" she asked. "What's that riggin' you're wearin'?"

Joanda answered in a small voice: "Teacher gave me a sort

of a permanent. She gave the other girls one too. She asked all the mothers but you, 'cause I was absent day before yesterday."

"Permanents cost money," said Mama. A hard look came over her face.

"This one's free," said Joanda, "she said so."

"And she gave you a *free* lunch too," Mama went on. "Ricky told me. Thinks we're pore, don't she? Hot lunches and permanents in school! We send you to school to git book-learnin', to study lessons. I guess I better go in and speak a piece of my mind to this teacher o' yours."

"Oh Mama, *don't!*" begged Joanda. "She's all right, she's nice . . . I *like* her . . . she jest does some funny things, that's all. You can't never tell what she's gonna do next."

But Mama would not listen.

Daddy took Lolly and Mama rushed into the school building, with Joanda and Ricky at her heels. Mavis and Steve joined a ball game that had already begun. The hall was empty and no one seemed to be around. Mama turned to Joanda and whispered nervously, "Where can I find her?"

"We'll have to look," said the girl.

They found Miss Fenton in the dining room, talking to Mrs. Bronson. She looked up in surprise as Mrs. Hutley came in followed by her two children. Mama's hair wasn't combed and she still had her apron on.

"What do you mean by making my children eat a free lunch?" demanded Mama. "Think we're too pore to pay for it?"

"Why, Mrs. Hutley," said Miss Fenton, "didn't the children tell you? We found cockroaches in their cold lunch yesterday. You wouldn't want them to eat it after that, would you?"

"Why, er . . . I s'pose not . . ." said Mama weakly. Then she began again. "And you gave Nannie a permanent . . ." Mama's bravado was rapidly fading away in these strange surroundings.

"I'll go and comb out Joanda's hair for you to see," said Miss Fenton, "while Mrs. Bronson shows you our new dining room." Joanda and Miss Fenton went out.

Mama looked at the cupboard full of groceries and the pots cooking on the stove. Suddenly her heart smote her — she had been depriving her children of good nourishment to build their bodies and give them strength. The food was better than she could give them at home. She didn't need to be told that. She looked around the pretty room while Mrs. Bronson explained everything.

"I never thought it was nice like this," said Mama. "Maybe they wouldn't get sick so much . . ."

Mrs. Bronson explained that the price of meals was charged for those who had big families and could not pay, and said there were funds to take care of that. No one need know they couldn't pay. She added, "You'll let them come, won't you?"

Mama nodded.

When she returned to Miss Fenton's room, there was Joanda with her hair combed out. It hung soft and naturally to her shoulders.

"I only cut off the stringy ends," said Miss Fenton. "Joanda's so pretty . . ."

"Purty, huh!" sniffed Mama. "She don't look no different from other young uns. I don't want her gittin' notions . . ."

"She's as pretty as a picture," said Miss Fenton, "and it won't hurt her to know it, either." She turned to a shelf of books at the back of the room. "We're starting a school library. We want to get more story books . . ."

"I thought they come to school to read outa *lesson* books," said Mama.

"Mama, Miss Fenton says I can take a book home with me and read it."

Mama shook her head. "We don't have no truck with books."

"Here's a pioneer story," said Miss Fenton. "You'll like it, Mrs. Hutley, when Joanda reads it to you. She's one of the best readers in the whole school and a prize speller too. She likes words and understands what they mean. She ought to read constantly."

At these words of praise, Mama flushed with pride, all her anger gone. Then she remembered she was keeping Daddy waiting. She thanked Miss Fenton and hurried out.

That evening Joanda ran all the way home. She could hardly wait to read the library book she carried under her arm.

◆　◆　◆

"Say, this is *good!*" said Joanda.

She was sitting on the back porch when Daddy came up. "What is?"

"It's a book, a pioneer story," said the girl. "I been lookin' at all the pictures. We've got a library at school, with story books to take home and read."

"I told that teacher my kids go to school to study *lesson* books," said Mama at the door.

"Come on in, let's see if I can read it," said Daddy. The children trooped in the house behind him. "Will you tell me the hard words if I get stuck, Nannie?"

"I sure will," said Joanda proudly.

Daddy sat down by the kitchen stove and began to read the book aloud. When he got tired, Joanda took his place. Mama went on getting supper while she listened. The children crowded close. Even Lolly sat very still.

The book told of hard work and courage and struggle. It had happiness, meanness and sorrow in it. At the sad parts they all cried. Daddy and Joanda read each evening after school until the end was reached.

"It sounds like real to me," said Daddy. "I feel like I know them folks somehow."

"That's 'cause they're just like us. They had the same troubles in them days too," said Mama. "We're not the only ones had it hard."

Spring had come to the cotton country and it began to rain every day. The dirt roads became mud-puddles and the banks of the ditches and bayous were running full. Daddy drove the children to school in the truck. Then one morning he was afraid he would stick the truck, so the children started for school on foot.

They had finished reading the library book the night before and Joanda was taking it back.

Joanda never knew just how it happened. Afterwards she wished she hadn't tried to lift Ricky over the mud-puddle. But he had no rubbers and she did. When she was halfway across, the book slipped out from under her arm.

"Oh! Oh!" she cried. Then she dropped Ricky and he got his feet muddy and wet, after all.

But it was the book that mattered. Joanda had told Miss Fenton she would take good care of it. Daddy had folded a newspaper around its beautiful blue cloth covers, so not a spot should get on them. He had turned the pages carefully. Each time after they finished reading, Mama had put the precious book up on a high shelf out of Lolly's reach. Joanda wanted to be sure to return the book to school as pretty and clean as when she borrowed it.

Now it had fallen in the mud-puddle. Horror-stricken, she reached down through the cold, slimy mud and brought it up. She held it out at arm's length.

"By golly, you'll ketch it!" cried Ricky. "Teacher will sure whoop the buttons off your dress for *that!*"

"I'm goin' home," said Joanda. "You go on to school. Hurry and you can ketch up with Steve and Mavis. They're waitin' at the corner."

Joanda walked slowly back, staring at the book, her heart sick within her. The whole family had loved every word and picture in the book and now she had ruined it. She knew Daddy hadn't any money to buy a new one to take its place. They were living on borrowed "furnish" now. She tried to open the pages which were stuck together with mud, but it was impossible. She stopped and thought awhile. She couldn't take the book home and she couldn't take it back to school.

She cut across the field, went to the top of the bayou bank and threw the book as far as it would go. It landed in the middle of the stream. She watched it slowly sink from sight.

The bayou was deep. She could never get the book again.

Then, panic-stricken, she ran home.

Back in the house, she sat down on a chair beside the stove. Mama questioned her, but all she said was: "I can't go to school any more."

Mama and Daddy decided she was sick and let her alone. It began to rain again. Daddy talked about the rain as he, too, sat by the stove.

"The field is a loblolly," he said. "If this keeps on, we'll never git the cotton planted. We ought to been breakin' ground two weeks ago. Most years we'd have our plowin' done by now."

"I was over to Lessie's yesterday," said Mama. "That gumbo mud gits on her chickens' feet and makes balls so big they can't walk. She has to ketch each one and knock the mud off."

"Why, when you walk in it yourself," said Daddy, "your feet git as big as a nail-keg! It takes you three hours to walk a mile and a quarter!"

He laughed, but Joanda didn't. Her face still had that stricken look.

"But gumbo land is best for cotton," Daddy went on. "It holds the moisture longer."

Mama looked out the window. "If it don't stop rainin', the house will soon be floatin' in water."

"Glad we don't live no nearer to Pemiscot by-o," said Daddy. He pronounced the word *bayou*: by-ō. "Them folks might have to git out in boats."

The days passed and it kept on raining. Joanda helped about the house and took care of Lolly. One day she made her a pair of jeans out of Steve's old pants. When she tried them on her, the girl brightened up and said, "She sure does look sweet with 'em on," and hugged and kissed her.

When Miss Fenton sent word home by Mavis, inquiring about the library book, Joanda refused to answer. Daddy and Mama both questioned her, but she told nothing. Mavis was unable to report to Miss Fenton, for the road got so bad, none

of the children could get to school. And there was no work
Daddy could do. So they all sat around in the house and waited for better weather.

"I sure wish you'd a brought us another of them good story
books to read, Nannie," said Daddy. "It would make the time
go faster."

Joanda frowned and said nothing.

At last the rain stopped, the sky cleared and the children
started back to school. All but Joanda, who refused to go.
Mama couldn't make her, so, in her easy-going way, said nothing and let her stay at home.

"Why, Joanda," said Aunt Lessie Burgess, dropping in one
day. "Why ain't you in school where you belong?"

Joanda dropped her eyes. "I don't like school."

"The road's too muddy," hastily explained Mama.

"But the other children walk," said Aunt Lessie. "It's not
too muddy for them."

"She ain't got rubbers or galoshes that fit her right," said
Mama.

"I'll send over some old ones of the twins'," said Aunt Lessie.
"They've outgrown them and they ought to be jest right for her."

"Don't you bother," said Mama. "She jest *don't like* this
school."

"But I thought she liked it so much," said Aunt Lessie. "She
was the best reader and the best speller, too, the twins told me."

"It's the teacher," said Mama. "She jest can't stand her."

"Why, all the kids are crazy about Miss Fenton," said Aunt
Lessie. "Jolene and Arlene say they'd rather have her than Miss
Tyler, but Miss Tyler's good too. We've got the two best teach-
ers we ever had at Delta Flats School this year."

"She does mighty funny things, that teacher does," Mama went on. "I never heard of such goin's on in any school before — this washin' their heads and cuttin' their hair and feedin' 'em we don't know what. And there's another thing. She don't learn 'em out of lesson books, she's gittin' story books . . ."

"They can learn out of them too," said Aunt Lessie. "Times are changing. The schools ain't what they used to be, but Miss Fenton's all right."

"Did you hear what she done?" asked Mama in a low voice. "*She put cockroaches in the cold lunch sacks.*"

Aunt Lessie chuckled. "Oh, I don't believe that."

"But Joanda saw her with her own eyes," said Mama.

"Did you, Joanda?" asked Aunt Lessie.

Joanda stared at the floor. She couldn't answer the question. She wished she hadn't told anybody, but Mama had pulled it out of her somehow. She wished the women would stop talking about her.

"Is it any wonder she hates her and won't go back to school any more?" said Mama.

"Well, she better forget it and go," said Aunt Lessie briskly. "Nannie's too smart a girl to be sittin' around here all day long doin' nothing. All the children are better off in school, now they got that hot lunch and everything up-to-date. My twins are fleshnin' up, they eat so much."

After the rains were over, the spring work began with a rush. As soon as the fields dried off, Daddy started working long hours, driving Big Charley's tractor, breaking ground. He came home barely long enough to eat and sleep.

One day after the roads were passable, a car came by and

the driver sounded the horn. Joanda was out at the pump, getting a bucket of water. Mama and Lolly hurried out the front door. Mavis and Steve and Ricky jumped out of the back seat of the car. Daddy was plowing the field next to the house. When Joanda saw Miss Fenton and Miss Tyler in the front seat she turned to run.

"Don't go, Joanda, " called Miss Fenton. "It's you I came to see. We are giving out garden seeds. Don't you want a couple of packets? What flowers do you like? Petunias? Nasturtiums? Prince's feather? Zinnias? Zinnias are so bright and pretty. They look nice in a bouquet to put on the table."

Joanda stood stiff like a stick of wood.

"How many do you want, Joanda?"

Joanda couldn't speak. No words would come.

"You'd have a pretty yard, if you'd clean it up and plant some flower beds," Miss Fenton went on. "Wouldn't you like to do that, Joanda?"

Mama, who was holding Lolly, came up closer to the car.

"This place don't belong to us, Miss Fenton," she said. "The boss-man and his wife wouldn't even thank us for it. They'd give us the dickens for doin' things like that."

Daddy came closer to the house with his tractor and its roaring drowned out the sound of voices. "Ricky! Come *here!*" Mama was terrified the boy would get in the way of the machine. "We don't want no more broken legs round here."

"You work for the Shands, don't you, Mrs. Hutley?" asked Miss Tyler.

"Yes ma'am," said Mama.

"They are friends of mine," said Miss Tyler. "I'm sure they'd be pleased if you took care of the place."

Miss Fenton looked at the tin cans, empty bottles, old rags and trash that littered the yard.

"Joanda, you're a big girl and you're not afraid of work. Why don't you rake up these tin cans and bottles and make your yard look nice?"

Still Joanda could not answer. She grasped the water bucket so tightly that her hand hurt.

"We've missed you at school, Joanda," Miss Fenton said gently.

"Next week on Friday, we're having Clean-Up Day," explained Miss Tyler. "The boys and girls are going to bring rakes and brooms and hoes and shovels. We're going to clean up the school yard so it looks as neat as a pin. We'll make flower beds and plant flower seeds. Won't you come and help us, Joanda?"

The girl shook her head. "Don't wanna come," she mumbled.

"We miss you very much, Joanda," repeated Miss Fenton. "Don't you want to pass to the next grade? If you are not sick, we will expect you back."

"It ain't hardly worth while now," spoke up Mama. "Cotton chopping time will soon be here."

"The cotton's just being planted, Mrs. Hutley," said Miss Tyler. "The children won't be chopping until June. School lets out long before that."

"Here's a packet of zinnia seeds, Joanda," said Miss Fenton, "and one of carrots. You can plant a row at the edge of the cotton field. This packet has a verse on it."

Joanda did not reach out her hand.

Daddy's tractor came close again. It turned the corner, and

roaring loudly, started off to the south. Joanda looked up to watch it. Then she saw Lolly out in the field behind it. The little girl was stumbling over the broken ground, calling to Daddy to give her a ride, but of course he could not hear her voice. She had on the new white shoes Daddy had bought her in town the previous Saturday.

Joanda flew. Her terror of the tractor was as great as her mother's. Daddy had come to a mud-puddle, pulled up and was about to back. He wanted to go through it fast so he wouldn't stick in it.

Joanda got there just before he backed. She took Lolly in her arms and held her tight. On her way to the house, she paddled her and told her not to go near the tractor. Lolly just laughed, but when she saw the mud on her new white shoes, she cried.

When Joanda got back, the teachers and the car were gone and Mama was in the kitchen. Joanda did not look at the seed packets until she had to set the table for supper. Then she picked them up and read the planting directions over.

"Want to hear the verse about carrots?" she asked.

"Sure do," said Mama.

Joanda read:

"'Carrots are rich in Vitamin A,
They'll make you strong for school or play;
They'll keep your teeth without decay,
And drive those horrid colds away.
So plant these seeds some time in May,
And you'll eat carrots every day.'

"I like that, Mama, don't you?" Joanda smiled as she hadn't smiled since the loss of the library book.

Some weeks later, on a Sunday, Uncle Shine appeared again. The Hutleys were eating dinner, when Trouble dashed out barking. There was the same old Ford and the same old man. The children clung to his hands and arms and pulled him in.

"We're not gonna let you go this time," said Ricky.

"We'll tie you to a tree and keep you here," said Joanda.

"I don't see any trees," laughed Uncle Shine, looking around.

"To a porch post then," said Steve.

"Jest in time for dinner, Uncle," called Mama. "You're invited this time."

All through dinner, the Hutleys talked about things that had happened to them since Christmas day. But Uncle Shine did not tell where he had been or what he had been doing. He just wanted to listen to Neva and her husband and children and to find out how they were getting along, he said. They took him out to see the cotton as soon as dinner was over.

"It's comin' up," cried Lolly. She ran into the field and tried to pull up a stalk but couldn't. Daddy laughed and said, "It sure is tough."

After the rains were over, the warm sun had come out and brought the cotton plants up, long rows of small green shoots, sprouting a few star-shaped leaves.

There was something hopeful about the sight. The annual ritual had begun again. Each year there was always new faith and hope that if the crop were good, the Hutleys — and thousands of other cotton farmers — could pay their debts and have a little over. They did not ask for much — only the security of a bare living.

Daddy and Mama and Uncle Shine and the children stood at the edge of the field and they looked down the long rows.

"Looks like a good season this year," said Daddy. "Not too wet and not too dry."

"If only the army worms and the red spiders and leaf worms would go somewhere else," said Mama. "All that rain we had will sure bring bugs."

"We're lucky not to have the boll-weevil," said Daddy. "The weevil gits froze out up here in northern Arkansas, our winters are so cold. The poor devils that have to fight the boll-weevil can't never make a good crop. Jest look at this good black delta soil."

"When I was a younger feller here," said Uncle Shine, "this was all woodland with virgin timber, and the lumber companies were just comin' in. The Mississippi River levee was always breakin' and causin' bad overflows. That's where your black soil came from — down that old river. When my Pa home-steaded up near the Missouri line, all his farm was under water except a ridge where he pastured his cows and horses. Long about 1914 when they began to grow the first cotton on new ground, it grew as high as a house, but was so weak it fell right over. Folks found out they had to grow corn for two or three years after clearin' the woodland, then plant cotton. Soil was too rich."

"They say this black soil won't never wear out," said Daddy. "Lucky for us. We don't pay a cent for fertilizer, 'cause we never put a drop on."

"Worst trouble we have is with grasshoppers," said Mama.

"They come in July and eat the cotton flowers and all the leaves. They come in droves from them ditch-banks along the bay-o."

"Soon as the old cotton goes to puttin' out leaves, we gotta go to choppin'," complained Mavis. "First time we chop, we gotta thin the plants in the row. Gotta chop it three times in all to get the weeds out."

"If we could jest be sure the price o' cotton would be good," said Daddy, "we'd work our heads off an' not mind it."

"Seems like a lot o' work for the little you get out of it," said Uncle Shine thoughtfully.

"I gotta make good this year," exclaimed Daddy, full of enthusiasm. "I wanta buy me some tools of my own. Big Charley's promised me the first tenant house that gits empty on his place."

"That's the way to talk!" said Uncle Shine. "Pull yourself up — there's no other way. Neva tells me you're a good carpenter. Is that so?"

"Oh, I do a little jack-leg carpenterin' when there's nothin' else to do," laughed Daddy, "jest between the jobs on the crop."

"I've bought me a little bungalow this side o' town," said Uncle Shine, "and I'm fixin' it over. I could use you in your spare time — day labor, you know."

"Oh, Uncle Shine! Are you gonna live there?" cried the children.

"Sure am," said the old man. "I'm tired of gallivantin'. I'm like the old horse — I've come home to roost, but not in a cotton field. I'd rather be near town."

The children clapped their hands. "And you'll come to see us every Sunday!"

"Maybe even during the week," laughed Uncle Shine.

It was Uncle Shine who suggested that Daddy start a bank account with the wages he paid him for his carpentry work. Uncle Shine kept on thinking of more and more jobs for him to do. He advised Daddy to get the full amount saved before making the purchase of the necessary tenant tools, so he would not have to pay more by buying in installments. Week by week Daddy's bank account began to grow.

One day Daddy came back from work, whistling gaily.

"What are you so tickled about, Daddy?" asked Joanda.

"Come and see what I brought, young un," answered Daddy.

The family crowded round as Daddy unloaded from the truck a white-painted door with a glass panel in it. He carried it up on the front porch.

"It's our'n!" he said with pride. "Uncle Shine bought hisself a newer fancier door, with an oval-shaped glass. He was goin' to throw this one out."

"Out! My goodness!" said Mama. "A good door with glass in it! What you fixin' to do? This ain't *our* house, Dave. The Shands won't like it. . ."

But Daddy already had the old door off its hinges and was fitting the new one in place. He told the boys to store the old door up in the loft, to be replaced if and when the Hutleys moved.

"'Cause this is *our* door," he added, "and when we move we'll take it right along with us. I'll give it another coat of white paint. Then, wherever we live, people will know it's the Hutleys' house, when they see the pretty glass door!"

Mama brought warm water and a cloth and washed the glass window on both sides. It looked very beautiful. It let in *light*. They all had to stand in the front room with the door shut to see how light it was.

Joanda looked at the newspaper-pasted walls. "If we could only have some pretty wallpaper . . ."

"And some new furniture," added Mama. "I keep thinking about that couch I picked out at Atkins' furniture store."

"And a couple of easy chairs to match," added Mavis.

"As if we ain't already got ten times too many places for our money," laughed Daddy.

They all went out in the road to see how the new door looked from the front.

"It makes the house look all *dressed up!*" cried Joanda.

"*All dressed up!*" echoed Lolly, clapping her hands.

"Steve," said Mama, "go git the rake. Let's clean up some of this trash. Why don't we make a dump in one place back by the shed, and stop throwing trash around? Let's have Clean-Up day here like at school."

Joanda looked at Mama, her face beaming. "Can I make some flower-beds and plant those flower seeds? And a row of carrots at the edge of the cotton field?"

Mama put her arm around her. "You sure can, sugar."

◆ ◆ ◆

"Ricky, go to the house and pump your bucket full of water," said Joanda. "Hurry now, we're thirsty."

The small boy sat down in the row. "I don't want to," he said. "It's too heavy when it's full."

"Git it half full then," answered Joanda, "but you'll have to go twice as many times." She watched him as he started down the long cotton row, walking slowly toward the red shotgun house.

The cotton had grown quickly. The plants were six weeks old and nearly six inches tall, which meant it was time to chop. While Daddy plowed corn for Big Charley, all the family took their hoes and went out to the field which bordered on the bayou bank.

Big Charley had arranged for the four Burgess children to chop too. He also brought two truckloads of Negro choppers of all ages out from town. They were working in a much larger field joining Daddy's fifteen acres — a long row of workers moving steadily across the field.

Big Charley's straw-boss came over and showed the children how he wanted the chopping done.

"Let two or three plants stand about twelve or sixteen inches apart," he said. "Clean out all the weeds between. A good cotton chopper stands straight and never bends over. He holds his hoe like a broom, reaching over the row and hoeing toward himself. Just walk along and keep hoeing as you go. Don't leave any long skips."

Joanda and the children listened and tried to do just at the man said. It was June now and the sun was hot. *Down, up, down, up,* the children walked along the rows swinging their hoes. The Burgess boys and Steve were soon far ahead. The Burgess twins kept abreast of Mama, Joanda and Mavis. Lolly played in the dirt.

Now and then a wave of made-up song from the Negro workers in the field was carried over the breeze: "*I's gwine to town . . . I's gwine to town . . . I's gwine to buy me a new hat and gown . . .*" Sometimes it was a hymn: "*Lord, I want to be like Jesus . . .* "

"Ain't cotton the purtiest stuff you ever saw?" asked

Joanda. "I jest like to look at it. I think ours is the purtiest in the county. It's growin' so fast, it's gittin' knee-high . . ."

"What's purty about cotton?" complained Mavis. "Before it gits knee-high, we gotta chop it again. All we do is chop, chop, chop!"

"*Chop, chop, chop,*" echoed Lolly. She was tired of her dirt pies now and began to throw dirt. She threw it over Mavis's head and in her eyes.

"Quit that, young un!" scolded Mavis. "You jest do that again and I'll set your clothes afire!"

"I'll take her back to the house," said Mama. "I don't feel good. I got to lie down awhile. Mavis, you tell the straw-boss when he comes."

Mama and Lolly walked back to the house. After a long time Ricky returned with the water. He went to all the choppers one by one and they dipped up water in the dipper and drank. Then the bucket was empty again.

"I can't find our lunch, Nannie," said Ricky.

"Where'd you put it?" asked Joanda.

"Down in the shade at the end of the row," said Ricky.

"But I told you not to leave it in the grass," scolded Joanda, "'cause it might could git antses all over it. Why didn't you put it in the boss's truck? Now I gotta stop work and go look for it."

Joanda and Ricky hunted through the tangled grass and weeds along the bayou bank. Soon they heard a dog growling.

"There's that old Trouble!" cried Joanda. "He's got our baloney and he's eatin' it."

"I'll whack him good!" Ricky chased the dog but could not catch him.

"That dog's always makin' trouble," said Joanda. "Ketchin' people's chickens, barkin' at cars, gittin' that salmon can stuck on his head, and now eatin' our baloney. Like Mama said, he sure was born for trouble, that's why she named him that."

"What are we gonna eat now?" asked Ricky.

"Go back to the house and git some more water," said Joanda. "Tell Mama, Trouble took our baloney. Maybe she'll give you something else for us to eat. Tell her we're powerful hungry."

The small boy trudged slowly across the field. Joanda wondered if she could wait until he made the long slow trip to the house and back again. She kept on chopping. Now she was far behind the others. *Down, up, down, up, down, up . . .* Her back began to hurt, so she straightened it. The trick was not to bend your back. She had heard Mama say that often and the straw-boss said so, too. The weeds had started growing, and the stems of the cotton plants were strong and wiry. It was hard to chop them off.

"Must Jesus bear the cross alone,
And all the world go free . . ."

She could hear the Negroes singing again. Their rich voices floated across the field. She rested her hoe to listen. She wished she could sing too, but chopping made her too tired.

Then she felt hungry again. Would Ricky never come? The others were all eating at the straw-boss's truck on the far side of the field. At last she heard Ricky calling and decided Mama wanted her to come to the house to eat. She dropped her hoe and ran to meet him.

"Mama wants you," said Ricky, panting. "She said tell Nannie . . . come quick . . . git Daddy . . ."

"Is Mama sick?" asked Joanda. "She was all right this morning." She wondered why Mama had left the field and where she could find Daddy.

She and Ricky ran to the house. She saw her the first thing. Mama was half-sitting, half-lying on the floor of the back porch, leaning against the wall of the building. She looked as if she had fallen there and could not get to her feet again. Her hoe lay on the steps. Lolly was making mud pies in the yard.

Mama tried to speak. "Git Daddy . . ." she gasped. "Gone blacksmith shop . . . have plow welded . . . Ricky . . . keep Lolly."

Daddy must have stopped on his way to the blacksmith shop to tell Mama where he was going.

Joanda was so frightened she could not think, but she knew she must act quickly. She told Ricky to hold Lolly so the little girl would not follow her. Then she ran down the road toward the corner. The blacksmith shop was at the garage next to Brownie's store. It was a mile from the Hutleys' house. It took a long time to get there.

As Joanda came up, she saw Daddy in his truck starting off. "Goin' to town to buy a new plow for Big Charley," he called. "Can't git the old one welded. What you doin' here? Why ain't you choppin', Nannie?"

"*Stop, stop! Wait!*" called Joanda frantically. "Mama's . . ."

Daddy stopped, picked her up and listened. "Sounds like a heart attack," he said. He turned around and drove quickly back to the house.

Mama was still leaning against the wall, gasping for breath.

With Joanda's help, Daddy carried her into the house and laid her on a bed. Lolly was screaming, but Ricky held her tight.

"You'll have to go git a doctor, Nannie," said Daddy. "Mama's bad off, she can't git her breath. I don't dare leave her. . . . Go back to the store, ask Brownie to git a doctor to come quick. Ask him to phone Brother Davis, too." Daddy put pillows under Mama's head and began to fan her. "She's smotherin' . . . go as fast as you can, sugar."

After Joanda left the house, Bug Burgess came up. "Hi there, Ricky, you ole water boy, where's our water?"

"That you, Bug?" called Daddy from inside. "Chase home and ask your mother to come fast as she can git here. My wife's dyin'."

"Gee, Mr. Hutley, I sure will." The boy dashed off.

The tears streamed down Joanda's face as she ran. She never knew how she managed to go that mile the second time, except that she flew on wings of fear. Her feet seemed never to touch the ground. Brownie took one look at her white face and put in the calls for her. He phoned Mrs. Shands too, and offered to go to town and bring Uncle Shine out.

Joanda wanted to hurry back but she couldn't. She was tired all over. Her feet were so heavy she could hardly lift them. When she was halfway home, Mavis came running across the field.

"You jest better git out here and chop cotton, Joanda Hutley!" she scolded. "The staw-boss was plumb put out when he saw you and Mama was both gone and he was two choppers short. I told him you went to bring us some water, 'cause I saw you runnin' off with Ricky. Where you been — down to the store buyin' yourself some candy? Where's our water? We're about to die . . . . We ain't had but one drink all day, and I got a terrible sideache. I always git the sideache . . ."

Joanda stood still and listened. She was too numb and tired and grief-stricken to reply. Fear clutched her heart again — maybe Mama had died. . . . She came to her senses, found her feet and ran to the house. Still scolding, Mavis went back to the field.

When Joanda got there, Aunt Lessie was in the room with Mama and soon the doctor came. He went into the house and closed the door. All the time that the doctor was there, Joanda sat on the back porch, saying rhymes to keep Lolly and Ricky quiet.

"Peter went a-fishin'
Caught a little tadpole,
Put it in the kitchen,
Took it off his pole.
Sang a little song,
Not very long —
Doodlum doodlum doo,
Now it's all gone."

"Say another one," begged the children. Joanda went on:

"What did the peacock
Say to the crane?
I wish by golly
We'd git some rain.

Creek's all muddy,
Pond's all dry,
Wasn't for the tadpoles
Everybody'd die."

Joanda danced Lolly up and down as she said this one:

"Oh, my little boy,
Who made your britches?
Mamma cut 'em out
And Daddy sewed the stitches."

Joanda always ended it with: "Who made your britches, Lolly?" and Lolly always answered. "*You* did, Nannie, you know you did."

After a while, Joanda heard a car and thought it must be Uncle Shine. But it was Brother Davis and Mrs. Shands. The doctor came out just then and spoke to them. The preacher went in, but Mrs. Shands stopped for a moment. "The doctor said he gave her a shot and she can breathe now," she told the girl. "Has she been bad off?"

Joanda nodded. "Yes ma'm."

"Now don't you worry, Nannie." Mrs. Shands put her arm around her. "We'll take care of your Mama," she said and hurried in.

It was after five that evening when Mavis came back from the field.

"You got it nice and easy," she said to Joanda. "Sittin' on the porch in the shade and holdin' the baby all day. Tightwad went all the way to *his* house to git us water."

"*Sh!*" Aunt Lessie came to the back door. "Don't make a sound or she'll git worse."

"What's the matter?" whispered Mavis.

"Mama's sick," said Joanda. "She like to died."

"Oh, Nannie!" Mavis fell into her sister's arms and it was Joanda who did the comforting.

Aunt Lessie and Mrs. Shands moved Mama's bed beside an open window so she could get fresh air. They sat up all that night with her. Toward morning they went home. Daddy didn't work the next day, but he sent the children to the field to chop as usual. The work must go on — cotton did not wait.

Joanda stayed home to take care of Ricky and Lolly. She kept wishing Uncle Shine would come, but he didn't. In the middle of the morning, Mama had another heart attack.

"Nannie," called Daddy. "You'll have to go phone that doctor again. Brother Davis too."

Joanda's face turned white, as fear shook her. This time Mama would die. Lolly cried and screamed for Nannie to pick her up, but Joanda turned a deaf ear. For the first time she realized how selfish and demanding the baby — no longer a baby, but a big girl of three — had become. Had her own devotion made her so? All the way down the road she heard Lolly screaming, and she hoped Ricky could quiet her.

A car came suddenly up from behind. In it were Jed and Maggie Sutton who lived seven miles farther out the road. They stopped and Joanda explained her errand. They said they would telephone the preacher and the doctor, so Joanda turned back.

It was sad to look at Mama, so white and worn, struggling so hard for breath. At last the doctor came, and after he gave her the shot, she felt better. The doctor stayed most of the day and came back that night. The women returned and did what they could to help. Brother Davis came and prayed.

On the third day, Uncle Shine came, and Joanda felt easier. He had been away and just found the note that Brownie had left under his door.

The first words Mama spoke were to Uncle Shine. "The Lord sure can whoop us when He gits at it," she said. "I don't know what I done to deserve this. I'll have to try to lead a better life . . ."

On the fourth morning Mama wanted to get up, but Daddy and Uncle Shine wouldn't let her. The women went home and Uncle Shine stayed to help so Daddy could go back to his plowing.

The doctor's advice was not cheerful. He said that if Mama had another heart attack she must be taken to the hospital. And he said Mama must not chop any more cotton.

"But how will the cotton git chopped?" asked Mama.

It was Big Charley, the boss-man, who came to the rescue. He brought twenty geese, and Daddy built a run for them along the side of the shotgun house. They were to be turned into those cotton fields that were fenced to eat weeds and Johnson grass, so the cotton would not have to be chopped. It was fun to watch them. Each goose took a row and worked all day long eating the grass. They went to their trough to get water to drink, then went back to eat grass again.

The first time the children drove them to the field, Trouble barked and scattered them. It took a long time to get them in at the gate.

That night the children had to bring them back. Ricky went

ahead to keep them on the turn-row. Joanda came behind, stick in hand.

"Hurry up!" yelled Ricky. "You're too slow."

"If I go fast, they git tired and sit right down and rest," said Joanda. "Then I have to pick 'em up and carry 'em."

"Ugh!" said Ricky. "I wouldn't. I'd be a-scared they'd bite me." He began teasing a big fat goose and soon she was chasing him. "Stop her, Nannie! Stop her! She'll beat me to death with them big old wings. Don't let her bite me."

Joanda came to the rescue with her stick and soon had the flock in order again.

"If any geese ever chase *me*," she said when they reached the iron pump, "I'm not gonna pump 'em a drop of water."

Daddy came up. "Then they'll die," he said, "and you'll have to chop twenty big acres of cotton."

"Oh, I'll pump! I'll pump!" cried Joanda.

Soon the children were calling the pump "the goose pump," because the geese drank so much water. Every evening Joanda and Ricky pumped enough "goose water" to fill the large trough Daddy had made for them. The geese lined up on both sides of it, and lifting their heads high after each sip, drank and drank.

"They drink it as fast as we pump it," cried Joanda. Ricky got mad and splashed water all over them, but it only ran off their backs.

One time the geese got loose and ran straight to the bayou and had a swim. The children had to chase them back.

"Mama, I wish I was a goose," said Joanda. "I'd like to swim in the by-o, it's so nice and cool down there."

"You'd change your mind if I got after you with a gun," said Mama. She was sitting up by the window every day now.

Joanda looked at her mother in surprise. "Are you fixin' to shoot the boss-man's geese?"

"Yes," laughed Mama, "if they don't hush their quackin' and stop gittin' so much dust in here. When they're in the pen, they keep runnin' up and down the fence all day long. They make more dust than a car on a dirt road, and it all comes in here. If I close the windows, I'll smother sure."

"Seems like geese just try theirself to make people mad," said Joanda thoughtfully.

"If they run by my window one more time, I'll shoot 'em every one!" declared Mama.

"Better wait till you can aim a little better, Neva," laughed Daddy.

"They pester us more than they help," said Mama.

"They don't do any sech of a thing," said Joanda stoutly. "If Daddy gits shet of the geese, he won't have *me* to chop the old cotton."

And so the Hutleys put up with the geese.

The children made up a game they called "geesy feathers." The yard was filled with feathers now. Joanda tied two or three of them on the end of a string. Lolly ran and pulled it, the feathers flying in the air above her. Ricky and Steve stuck feathers in the soft ends of corncobs, pitched them up in the air and sailed them. The goose feathers were fun, and because of the geese, the children went back to school again.

The summer session at the split-term school opened on July 15th, to run to the end of August. Joanda's sorrow over the lost library book was now a thing of the past. She was eager to go to school again. It was hot in the schoolhouse in mid-summer, but not as hot as out in the cotton field.

It was good to be back. There were three shelves full of good library books to read; there was the pretty lunch room, and there was Miss Fenton. Joanda was glad it was not a new teacher. She had so much to tell her.

"I brought you some zinnias, the last ones," she said shyly, handing out a small bouquet. "I put two old tires around the flower-beds to keep Trouble off, but the mean ole geese trampled 'em down."

"Geese?" asked Miss Fenton.

"After Mama's two heart attacks, she couldn't chop cotton any more," Joanda explained. "I couldn't either, and we got way behind. So the boss-man brought geese to eat the Johnson grass. The doctor says Mama has to have all her teeth pulled. She's got malaria too . . . "

"I'm sorry," said Miss Fenton.

"That library book . . . the one I took home. . . ." Joanda dropped her eyes. It was hard to go on, but she knew she must. "I dropped it in a mud-puddle and messed it up . . . so I jest threw it in the by-o. . . . That's why I couldn't come back to school."

It was out now, and she felt better.

"But now you are back, and I'm glad."

Miss Fenton put a comforting arm around her.

Sarah Whitcher's Story

Elizabeth Yates

"Sarah!" Pa's voice was as sharp and clear as the sound of his ax when it bit into a tree. And it meant one thing.

Putting down the wood chips with which she was playing, Sarah trotted toward the cabin. Ollie, the big black dog, loped along beside her.

Pa stood in the doorway, the dinner horn in his hand. The other children had quickly responded to the sound of the horn, but it always seemed to take Pa's voice to get Sarah.

She ran to him. With one swift move, he scooped her up in his arms and she rode on his shoulder the rest of the way.

"What were you doing?"

"Building a cabin, like the kind you built for us."

"Didn't Ollie tell you it was time for noonday meal?"

"Ollie was asleep."

They went into the cabin and Pa set Sarah down on the bench by the trestle table, where the rest of the family was gathered.

"Seems we always have to wait for Sarah," eleven-year-old Reuben grumbled.

110

Joseph, younger by a year and quick to copy Reuben in everything, frowned at his sister. Little John, eight years old and hungry, drummed his spoon on the table.

"Children," Ma said gently, "that's no way to act on the Sabbath." Her hand, just touching the cradle near one end of the table, continued to rock baby Henry.

"But we're hungry, Ma," wailed five-year-old Betsey.

Ollie squeezed himself under the table to lick one bare foot after another of the several swinging there, then he settled himself for sleep.

As soon as Pa sat down, heads bowed and hands stilled as each one waited for him to speak the blessing.

"We're thankful, Lord, for all the good things you've given us, and we'll eat this food to grow strong in your service. Amen."

The "Amen" in which everyone joined was all but lost in the sound of wooden spoons against wooden bowls.

Sunday was different from other days in more ways than its food, not only in the Whitcher cabin near the crest of Pine Hill, but in every home that made up the settlement of Warren. Work was set aside in forest, field, and household.

Joseph interrupted his eating long enough to ask, "Why do we say thanks for this food? We said thanks for it yesterday when it was hot, now it's cold."

Pa's answer was brief and not to be questioned further, as his words came from the Bible. " 'In everything give thanks.' "

Most of the hundred or so people of the township lived in cabins in clearings on the mountain slopes. Only a few lived in the valley through which the Baker River ran. There, at the crossing of wagon tracks and bridle paths, was a gristmill where the settlers brought their wheat to be ground, and a sawmill for their logs; but no place for Sunday worship. Until a meetinghouse was built, each family kept the Sabbath in its own way. Horses might neigh, cattle low, sheep bleat, hens cackle, but no sound of work would be heard.

Reuben had asked his father why this was so, and the answer had been as certain as all Pa's answers. "It's a rule of life. Six days we work from sunup to sundown; on the seventh we rest."

"But not from sunup to sundown."

"Not quite," his father had agreed, smiling at Reuben.

There were always some necessary chores that had to be done, even on Sunday. Everyone helped with them and, since they were few, a good part of the day remained for each one to spend as he liked. That part began for the Whitchers after the noon meal when Pa read aloud from the Bible.

Wooden bowls were soon emptied, noggins of milk were drained, and all put in a basket to be taken later to the brook for washing. Then the family drew up in a loose circle by the slumbering ashes on the hearth. There was no need for a fire, but this was always the chosen place for reading and listening. Warm as the June weather was, ashes would never be allowed to get completely cold, as fire was part of the life in a settler's cabin.

Ma picked baby Henry up and nestled him in her arms. Betsey sat near, leaning against Ma's skirts. Joseph and Reuben sat back to back. Little John took his favorite place near the chimney. Hands that on other days might have busied themselves with carding or whittling were folded in laps or sunk deep in pockets. Sarah lay on the floor beside Ollie. Snuggling against him, she let her fingers move in and out of his shaggy hair.

"What you going to read to us, Pa?" Joseph asked as he watched his father take the big Bible down from its shelf.

"We've reached the Book of Job and that's where we'll begin today."

Pa read the first two chapters. Job was a good man and Pa understood him. He had a fine wife and family, land and stock, but the story didn't begin until Satan told God that Job wouldn't be such a good man if the Lord hadn't been so kind to him. God gave Satan a chance to test Job and one calamity after another happened. Soon Job had nothing left. Satan wanted to have another chance at testing Job's goodness and trust in the Lord. God told Satan to do what he liked but to spare Job's life.

"Job must have been a sight," Pa looked up from the page. "Poor now, without a home, covered with boils, and he must have felt mean. Even his wife told him to give up." Pa looked down at the page and read again, " 'What? Shall we receive good at the hand of God, and shall we not receive evil?' That was what Job said to his wife."

"Did he die, Pa?" Reuben asked.

"He did not. What kind of a story would that be?" Pa's hands were turning the pages quickly. The children liked it when he skipped to get on with the story.

"Three of his friends came to see him, and then a fourth," Pa went on. "They talked and talked because they thought Job had brought his troubles on himself. Job had plenty to say, too, but he never said anything against the Lord."

"What happened?"

"Listen. Here's the best part of the book. It begins at the thirty-eighth chapter and it goes right on to the end. 'Then the Lord answered Job out of the whirlwind — ' " Pa read with as much gusto as if the Lord had been speaking directly to him.

Sarah stopped playing with Ollie's hair to watch her father. The three boys stared at their father. Ma looked across the baby's face and the top of Betsey's head to rest her eyes on her husband, watching as well as listening.

" 'Then Job answered the Lord, and said, I know that thou canst do everything.' " There were only a few more verses and Pa read more slowly to make them last. " 'The Lord gave Job twice as much as he had before . . . and blessed the latter end of Job more than his beginning.' " When the story was over, Pa said, "It's sure enough that the Lord can do great things."

Ma sighed. "It's a wonderful story, John," though when she said it she was not certain whether it was the words or the way her husband read them that made them go so deep within her.

"But," Joseph looked at Pa, "what did Job do?"

"He trusted, son. No matter what happened, he knew the Lord would make everything come out right."

"And he did," Sarah said, though more to Ollie than to anyone else.

The closing of the book was the signal for dismissal, but Pa kept it open, so the children waited.

"Ma," he said, looking at her over the boys' heads, each one with hair as red as his own, "let us walk up to the Summit to see Chase and Hannah."

Pleased at the prospect, Ma nodded.

"We'll be back by sundown," Pa looked at Reuben, "so see that the stock is cared for and fed. Joseph, have an eye to the

114

fire, see that the ashes don't get cold and that there is wood on the hearth for the night. Little John, you are to mind the ones younger than yourself — Betsey, Sarah, the baby. Ollie will help."

"Yes, Pa," the boys chorused.

After the Bible was put away, Pa placed his big muscular hand on the head of one boy after another. It was not the first time he had given them such a charge. They accepted it, each one aware of his particular responsibility. Then they ran out of the cabin to follow their own pursuits.

"Betsey," Ma turned her attention to her daughter. "See that the bowls and spoons are washed, take good care of baby Henry, and watch that Sarah doesn't get into any trouble."

"Yes, Ma." Betsey received the baby from her mother's arms. Proudly and carefully, she carried him to the cradle.

Sarah, standing by the hearth with one arm around Ollie pleaded, "Want to go with you."

"No, Sarah." Ma was firm. "You must stay with the others. Ollie will play with you if the boys are too busy, and we'll bring something nice home to you all." Ma reached for her wicker basket. She never went away without it, as there was always something to be found that would be good to eat or to use or to look at.

Pa picked Sarah up and held her high in the air. She was a redhead, too, but the only one in the family with his pale blue eyes. Sometimes, when he looked into them, he felt that he was seeing his own in a glass. The others had their mother's dark eyes, and Betsey had her mop of brown curls. He set Sarah down on the doorstep, seized Ma's arm in the joy of the day and her company, and they were off. Walking briskly up to the

115

ridge, never once looking back, they ran as the path dipped down to Berry Brook.

Ollie pushed himself against Sarah, their heads almost on a level as they stood together in the doorway. From the back side of the cabin came the sound of the boys' voices. Ollie slathered his tongue over the face near his muzzle, then moved slowly away, swinging his tail as he brushed by Sarah and went around the cabin to join the boys.

Sarah, moving as quietly as Ollie and keeping close to the cabin wall, followed him. When she reached the corner she peeked around it to see what the boys were doing. Absorbed in their work, they were attaching disks of wood Pa had planed for them to some boards they had nailed together to make a cart.

"As soon as we get this done," Reuben was saying, "we'll make Ollie draw it."

Little John was fashioning a harness from some scraps of leather. "Ollie," he called, "come here to me so I can see if this fits you."

Sarah decided there was no game here in which she could play, so she backed away from the cabin corner to see what Betsey might be doing.

Standing in the doorway and watching Betsey, she soon realized that Betsey was far too occupied to be interested in a game. Baby Henry, sobs become screams, had demanded attention and Betsey's hands were full with him and his needs.

"You're wet, Henry, as wet as if you'd sat in Berry Brook but you'll have to stay as you are until I find something dry for you." Betsey crossed the room to Ma's big chest to find a change for Henry.

Everybody was busy. Everybody had something to do. Except Sarah.

She turned around and watched a bird hopping along the path in front of her. It stopped, scratched at the ground, then cocked its head at her. "Come along with me," it seemed to say as it took wing and flew into the nearby woods.

Sarah decided to pretend she was Pa when he first came to Pine Hill. He would have had an ax in his hand and she could not have one. His ax was almost as long as she was tall and she had never lifted it, but she could find a pretend-ax.

Hunting for a piece of wood, she followed the bird. As soon as she found a stick that was the right size and that fitted her hand nicely, she was no longer Sarah, but Pa, and the story he had told so often began to come alive in her.

It was all a long time ago when Pa lived in Salisbury, many miles to the south. He was a big man and he wanted mountains around him, so one day he told Miss Sarah Marston that he was off to the high country to find good land and build a tight cabin. Sarah stopped and addressed herself to a birch tree.

Pretending she was Pa, she spoke to it as if it were Ma. She stood very straight and shifted the ax to her left hand so she could hold out her right to the tree. She bowed and said to the tree in a deep bold voice, "You'll be willing to change the hills for the mountains, won't you, Miss Marston?"

A shiver of wind in the leaves might have served as an answer, but Sarah wanted to make her own. She put down the stick and went to stand with her back against the birch tree.

Now she was Ma. She ran her hands down her skirt to smooth it, as Ma would. Putting one leg behind the other, she dropped a curtsey and in a high polite voice said, "Yes, Mr. Whitcher, I'll exchange anything but you."

Sarah stepped away from the tree and picked up the stick. She was Pa again, ax in hand, marching off to the mountains, head high, free arm swinging. Before she had gone far she turned for one more sight of the birch tree. "I'll be back," she said in as deep a voice as she could manage.

A year had gone by before Pa returned to Salisbury. He brought Ma the news that he had cleared land and built a cabin in the settlement of Warren, where the mountains were big and the streams cold and six other families had their homes.

It made Sarah feel brave and strong as she thought of all that Pa had done on Pine Hill.

She stopped for a moment to get her bearings, as she had often known Pa to do when she was with him, then she marched on down the slope and waded into Berry Brook. The feel of the cold water was good, but she did not stand in it for long, for she was Pa and there was work to do.

On the far side of the brook the trees grew so tall they seemed to touch the sky. She found her way among them, skipping sometimes over the pine needles and patches of moss; running often as there was no underbrush to catch at her and hold her back. Now and then she stood still and tilted her head to look up to the sky, but the branches of the trees met high above her and she could not see the sky through their thick green.

After a while she came to a clearing where wild grasses grew. There were flowers among them and Sarah decided to pick some to take home to Ma. While she was picking, she saw something growing low on the ground that was even better than flowers.

Strawberries! Thick as stars in the sky, they spread over the ground, especially where the grass was thin. Sarah reached down to pick one. The taste was ripe and sweet. Putting down her bunch of flowers and the stick, she picked and ate strawberries until she was full. Then she thought to pick some for Ma.

She had nothing to put them in, so she tried to make a basket of grasses as she had often seen Ma do. But the grass was slippery. She could not make the stalks stay together, even the knots she tied wouldn't hold. Sarah picked up her bunch of flowers and looked for the stick, but couldn't find it. It had disappeared.

"I don't need it now," she said to herself. It had been an ax to cut down trees to make a clearing and build a cabin, but there were no trees here. Pa would like this sunny meadow for the stock. Ma would like it for its flowers and berries. Now she felt she could not get home quickly enough to tell them both about it.

The sun, poised on the tip of a near mountain, dipped slowly from sight. Clouds that had been gathering in the west began to move over the sky, and there was meaning in their grayness. Oncoming night and threatening rain were always reasons to seek shelter. Sarah, aware of the difference since the sun had gone, started to run toward the big trees.

It was darker among them than it had been in the clearing. Sarah ran more quickly until she was out of breath. She stopped for a moment and realized that she had not gotten anywhere. The forest was still all around her with its tall trees and the wind sighing through them. She listened, but she could not hear the sound of Berry Brook that would tell her she was nearing home.

"Pa!" she called.

Rain started to patter on the leaves high above her head.

◆   ◆   ◆

As dusk came to the cabin with rain fast following it, Joseph and Reuben piled logs on the fire. Little John set the tin lantern in the open doorway. Henry, deprived of his mother too long, began to whimper. Betsey did her best to comfort him.

Standing in the doorway just back of the lantern, the three boys peered into the night.

"Could be the rain came sooner up at the Summit," Reuben suggested as explanation for his parents' lateness.

"Could be the path downside the Oliverian is slippery," Joseph added.

"Could be — " Little John could think of no reason, so he threw his arms around Ollie and hugged him.

Then out of the night came the sound they were hungering to hear — Pa's mighty shout. The boys answered with a chorus of shouts and Ollie barked excitedly. Soon, from the darkness of the woods and into the thin track of light made by the lantern, Pa and Ma could be seen. Stepping quickly as they came down from the ridge, they hurried to approach the shelter of the cabin.

"What made you leave Sarah up at the Summit?" Reuben asked, when he saw there were only two and not three people come back home.

"We didn't leave her. She wanted to come, but she was told to stay home."

"Sarah's not here — " Joseph began.

"Sarah hasn't been here all afternoon," Reuben added.

Silence fell over them all. Betsey started to cry. Ma set her basket of berries on the bench by the door and reached quickly to gather the baby in her arms lest Betsey drop him. Little John, remembering now that he had been given the charge of the younger children, held himself tight against the shame and fear that gripped him.

"Is Sara lost?" Ma turned to Pa.

His face was stern and his lips were drawn tight together. "If she's strayed we'll soon find her." He addressed his wife as if no one else were present, and he said four words she would not forget, "Trust in the Lord."

The baby started to wail. Ma held him closer, patting him comfortingly. She looked up and over Henry's head to give her husband the wisp of a smile. All the years she had known him she had never doubted his word. She would not doubt it now.

Pa looked at the children, calling their names one by one and drawing their eyes to him.

"Reuben, get the dinner horn and blow it hard. One long blast, then count ten before you sound it again."

"Yes, Pa."

"Joseph, go to the Richardsons' and tell them we need help."

"Yes, Pa. And on down to the Patches'?"

Pa nodded. "Betsey, have a care for what Ma wants you to do. If we don't find Sarah soon, we'll be needing something to eat." He turned away and started out into the night, then drew back as a spate of wind-driven rain spattered against the cabin. "It's a warm rain," he said, "and gusty. It won't last long."

Little John tugged at his father's breeches, then buried his head against them. "Pa, tell me what I can do, please, Pa."

"Stay here, son." The big hand reached down to steady the heaving thin shoulders. "I'm going out to look for Sarah."

Pa left with the lantern. Calling Sarah's name constantly, he searched both sides of Berry Brook, particularly the places where Sarah used to play, and the deep pools below the waterfalls where she had often helped her mother with the washing.

Standing a few paces away from the cabin, Reuben blew the dinner horn with all his strength. He knew that the sound, echoing in a series of long circling halloos, could be heard at a great distance. Late as it was, and raining, those who heard could and would respond.

Joseph raced down the hill to the nearest cabin, shouting as he approached. "Sara's lost — lost."

Samuel Richardson asked no questions. He bade his wife keep an eye to the children and walked out of his cabin and up the slope to the Whitchers.

Hearing the sound of the horn, Joseph Patch stepped from his cabin in time to greet Joseph Whitcher.

"Is it fire, boy?"

"No — " Joseph fought hard to get breath enough to speak. "It's — Sarah — she's — lost."

Joseph Patch turned to his wife with a few words, then followed the boy into the night.

Within an hour nine men had arrived to join the search. Some answered the urgent blasts of the dinner horn, others heard the news as it raced from cabin to cabin.

"We'll soon find her," they said to assure Ma and the children.

"Those little legs couldn't go too far."

Calling to each other, calling to Sarah, some worked slowly

over the area within a half mile of the Whitcher cabin. They looked under brush, in hollows, by stumps and fallen logs. They held their lanterns toward any shelter where a child might have curled up in sleep. Some went much farther.

While they were gone, Ma and the boys built up a fire in the open space outside the cabin; then she sent them all to bed. They protested, but Ma was firm.

Betsey asked if she could have the cradle beside her. "I don't want baby Henry to get out of my sight."

Ma laughed, to cheer herself as much as the children. She hugged Betsey. "Henry can't walk a step, but he may need watching all the same."

Little John lingered. "Ma, I'll keep my eyes on everyone in the cabin."

"Get some sleep, too, Little John. There'll be work for us all tomorrow."

Ollie followed the children and Ma heaped more wood on the fire.

Pa, returning from his search that had yielded nothing, met two of the men at Berry Brook.

"We've been as far as the big boulder," one said.

"She couldn't have got that far!"

"She just might," the other replied, "but that's a varmint's den. She wouldn't have stayed there long."

Pa tried to be cheerful. "She's sleeping somewhere. Come and dry yourselves by the fire."

The nine men stood around the fire with Ma and Pa, telling where they had gone, blaming their disappointment at not finding Sarah on the dark, and vowing they would find her as soon as morning came.

"Yes," Pa agreed, "we'll do better hunting with daylight to aid us, and a turn in the weather." He tilted his head to catch the direction of the breeze. "Wind out of the north will soon clear the rain away."

One by one the men took up their lanterns to return to their homes. "We'll be back in the morning."

Ma said, "I'll sit by the fire, John. You'll need rest for tomorrow. Take it under cover."

"How about yourself?"

"I'll watch for Sarah."

Pa heaved two more logs on the fire, logs that would be good for several hours' burning, then he left her. Once inside the cabin he took a quilt from the chest and spread it on the floor by the hearth. Through the open door he could see his wife outlined by the fire and beyond her the dark boles of the trees. Somewhere in those woods his daughter was sheltered.

Determinedly he closed his eyes. Ma was right, a man needed sleep if he was to do his work well the next day; but Pa had long ago trained himself to sleep light. Should a sound be heard, he could spring quickly into action.

The night had many sounds for Ma and at each one she alerted. When there was a whispering at the edge of the woods she ran quickly toward it, stumbling in the darkness once she had left the circle of light. "Sarah, Sarah," she called, as she held her arms out to embrace her child.

There was no reply and Ma had to admit to herself that the sound was only that made by leaves in the movement of the wind.

Another time she strained her ears, for the rippling of Berry Brook was like little Sarah's laughter. She wanted to plunge into the dark and find her way down to the brook, but she told herself that a child would scarcely be laughing at such an hour.

Glancing toward the cabin, she saw her husband stretched out in sleep by the warm ashes. After awhile she crept into the cabin to see if the children were sleeping soundly. The three boys were in the trundle bed. Betsey, at one side of the big bed, had an arm resting on the rim of the cradle that held the baby. Somewhere Sarah was sleeping, too, Ma told herself, and by the time another night had come around she would be safe in the bed beside her sister. The thought cheered Ma and she returned to sit by the fire. Yearning for morning, she threw sticks on to brighten the blaze, thinking light would speak to light and so hasten the coming day.

At last the long silence was broken by a bird calling in the woods. Soon there was an answering call, then the forest came alive with song, chatter, rustlings. Light began to filter through the trees. Blackness gave way to grayness. Strange shapes became old familiars. Sheep bleated for pasture, the cow lowed to be milked, hens cackled for feed.

"Reuben! Joseph! Little John!" Pa called the boys.

Startled out of sleep, Reuben responded first. "Is Sarah home?"

Joseph and Little John sat up. "Is she here? Is Sarah here?"

Pa shook his head. "Not yet. Come along out and help me with the stock."

Ma drew a bucket of water from the well. Some she tipped into a basin on the bench by the cabin door, the rest she carried to the hearth to commence preparations for the morning meal. Henry whimpered.

"Bring him to me," Ma said to Betsey. "He'll be hungry and wet. I'll care for him. Make yourself ready for the day."

Soon they had drawn up to the trestle table. Wooden bowls had wild strawberries in them which Ma had brought back from the Summit; even the wooden bowl at the empty place.

Pa gave thanks. "For what You've given us. For the care You're taking of Sarah. Amen."

Under the table Ollie moved among the feet, licking each one in turn.

"Did you get the berries at Uncle Chase's?" Joseph asked.

"Yes, the field in front of their cabin was red with them."

"Was that what made you so late getting home?"

"Yes," Ma said, "I picked longer than I should."

Before they had finished, Uncle Chase stood in the doorway. "Whatever help you need, I'm here to give it."

Pa motioned his brother to sit at the empty place, and while he ate told him what had happened.

Word about the Whitchers' lost child had traveled all over the Township of Warren. Every man who could leave his work wanted to join in the search. So sure was one farmer of finding Sarah within a short time that he left his oxen yoked in the field. Another hung his scythe over the limb of a tree, certain he would be handling it soon again and could finish his swale before dusk.

Confident and high-spirited, they tramped up the bridle path from Warren, up the slope of Pine Hill to the Whitcher cabin. Some carried axes, two had long-barreled guns, each wore a dinner horn for signaling. The day was bright and warm. The men laid wagers with each other.

"I'll give John Whitcher one of my suckling pigs if we don't find the little girl before noon."

"I'll plow any man's field for him if we don't have her at sundown."

By the time Pa, accompanied by Joseph and Reuben, returned from their search of the nearby woodland, twenty men had arrived at the cabin. They were all men of Warren. Some came from Beech Hill in the southerly part of the township, others from Height-o-Land to the north; three came from Runaway Pond and two from Patchbreuckland. All were known by name as neighbors; the Whitchers greeted them as friends.

Before setting out, Pa made sure they were familiar with the signals. "Three short sharp blasts in quick succession will give the good news that Sarah has been found," he said, "but we'll blow a single blast at intervals to keep us all in touch."

The men nodded. They knew the signals well. Then they were off.

Ma, standing in the doorway of the cabin with the baby in her arms and the four children near, waved.

"They'll find her, won't they, Ma?" Little John begged.

"They'll find her. We'll all be sitting together around the hearth by nightfall and your father will be telling us a story. But you three boys have his work to do, so you'd best get started. Betsey, I'll need your help if I'm to have something for those men to eat when they return. They'll be hungry."

The boys went toward barn, pasture, vegetable patch to do the work Pa would have done with their help and now they had to do without him. Before they had gone far, Ma cried after them, "When I call your names, you're to call back."

"Yes, Ma," they chorused. Each one realized as never before the importance of keeping in touch.

Over the outside fire an iron cauldron had been slung, and in it a meal would soon be simmering. When Ma needed more wood she called to Little John. "Finish that last row you're hoeing and then get me some wood for this fire."

"Yes, Ma, and I'll put it in the cart so Ollie can help."

When Little John finished his row he whistled to Ollie. Between the two of them, wood for a day's burning was brought and stacked within easy reach for Ma to put on the fire.

Led by Pa and Uncle Chase, the twenty men formed into two groups and fanned out into the woods, calling Sarah's name and signaling to each other at agreed intervals. Pa took his group down through the maple stand to Black Brook and Kelly Pond. Every imaginable place was searched, but not so much as a single clue — footprint or tatter of clothing — was discovered.

The group took counsel together and reluctantly agreed that this was not where Sarah had wandered. Willingly they followed their leader up the long climb past Oak Falls to Wachipauka Pond under the Webster slide. Resting by the shore of the pond, they blew long slow blasts as they called to the other searchers and to the little girl. The mountain wall gave back a sobbing echo.

"Where now, John?"

"Back to the cabin, searching as we go."

The descent was slow and difficult, giving them plenty of time to study the wilderness of rocks around them before they gained the cooling shade of the forest.

Uncle Chase took his group up the course of the Oliverian. Stopping to drink from one of its many pools, where the clear water revealed the shapes and colors of the stones over which it ran, more than one man had the same thought. A child stopping to drink or play, and losing balance, would soon be swept downstream by the force of the current. So they looked where the water swirled and turned in its course, but no one reported any kind of trace. They followed the Oliverian through a deep part of the forest to the foot of Moose hillock on the far easterly side of the township.

Uncle Chase knew every tree, every boulder; even the darkest passes on the side of the mountain were familiar to him. Ten years ago he had been the first white settler to climb to the peak in pursuit of game, and soon after he had built his home in a lap of the mountain that commanded a wide sweep of the valley.

"No child could ever go this far," a man said, shaking his head wearily.

"I've been a hunter as long as I've been a man," Chase replied, "and there's no telling where anything alive might go."

But there was no more clue for those who searched on the rugged easterly side of the township than there had been for those who searched on the more settled westerly part.

At sundown the two groups met at the cabin. Ma stood ready to give them the food that had been simmering through the day in the big cauldron, but her smile of welcome faded when she realized that there was no man among the twenty who had anything to report.

Pa went toward her. "We're all hungry."

Bowls were filled and soon emptied; few words were

spoken. As the men turned away to go to their own homes, each one went up to Ma and gave the only comfort in his power to give, "We'll be back with the light."

That night Joseph and Reuben kept watch by the fire and Ma rested in the cabin. Only by being near Pa could she be sure that he would take the sleep he needed after his long day and before another one to follow.

The three youngest children were soon asleep; the two older boys spelled each other as they kept the fire. Ma felt restless. It was easier to bear anguish during the day when there was work to put the hands to. Darkness filled her mind with pictures of all the things that might have happened to Sarah.

Pa stood beside her and put his arms around her.

"She's so small," Ma sobbed against Pa's shoulder.

"Sarah is big for her years and she's got good sense."

"But — but — "

"Every man in the countryside is doing what he can to help find Sarah," Pa said in the low tone of voice that he used when he gentled an animal. "The Lord will find a way to help us all."

Ma nodded. Pa trusted the Lord; she would have to trust Pa.

"We'll find her tomorrow," Pa promised.

◆ ◆ ◆

Next morning the twenty men of Warren were joined by as many more, for the news was spreading over the mountains and down into the valleys. Some who came from far rode horses that had been taken from shafts or plows. One man who came all the way from Newbury on the west side of the Connecticut River rode a white horse who had recently foaled. Beside the dam trotted the little filly, who was interested in everything but in nothing so much as nuzzling from the mother.

"A white horse is a lucky sight!" exclaimed Mrs. Patch, who had come with her husband to stay with Ma while the men were away.

Betsey, standing near, heard the words and slipped her hand into Ma's. "Two white horses must be very lucky."

"One of them's just a foal," Ma cautioned.

"But it will be a horse someday," Betsey insisted, "and it is white."

"We're from Wentworth," the spokesman for a group of new arrivals said.

"I'm from Romney, and my two brothers here come from Orford."

"We're from Piermont."

"The men of Haverhill have yet to find their match," a powerful man with a voice as big as his body shouted.

Pa and Uncle Chase welcomed them all and gave them directions. Samuel Richardson and Joseph Patch were designated additional leaders. Now there were four groups taking the points of the compass to penetrate the forest. Areas already searched would be searched again and communication would be constant.

"A dinner horn on Moose hillock can be relayed to a party near the Webster slide within minutes," Uncle Chase said, "and the first man to send the three short sharp blasts into the air will be — "

"Our man!" roared a dozen voices.

So they went off, some boastfully, some doggedly, all hopefully; but ears craving to hear the three sharp blasts went hungry. Only the low slow sound that kept contact wailed repeatedly through the mountains during the long hours of the second day of the search.

That sunset, as they gathered before the Whitcher cabin and Ma with Mrs. Patch's help ladeled food into wooden bowls, the last man in came running down from the ridge.

"Footprints!" he shouted. "I've seen footprints in the sand along Berry Brook not a mile from where we're standing."

All eyes turned on him.

"Footprints?" The word ran through the group; with some it was an exclamation, with some a question.

"A child's?" Pa asked.

The man nodded, glancing from Pa to Ma.

Betsey smiled up at Ma and whispered, "Two white horses are going to be very lucky."

"Beside the child's footprints were the paw prints of a bear." He splayed his right palm and pressed it to the earth to give some indication of size.

There was silence.

"She's been torn in pieces," one of the men said.

"She's eaten up," another agreed.

Ma put her apron up to her face to catch a sob, then she drew the children closer to her. Ollie whimpered and Joseph threw his arm around him.

"If it's a she-bear," Uncle Chase spoke slowly, "like as not the child will be unharmed."

The meal was soon finished. Then the men turned away, but not before they had said, "We'll be back with the light."

Down the hill to their cabins went the men of Warren, while

those who had come from a distance made camp in the woods and vowed they would be the first to start on the search when morning came.

"The news has got to Plymouth now," Samuel Richardson said as he mounted his horse to get back as quickly as possible to chores that generally demanded a day and now must be done in a single hour of dusk.

"If the news gets to Concord and the militia come to Warren to join the search, I doubt that they'd find her even then," one of the men from Piermont murmured, though he had no intention of giving up the search.

Wednesday was a day like the other two, bright and fair; men went into it with hope, spurred on by the clue of the footprints. The area near where they had been seen was gone over and over, but nothing more came to light. The clue proved to be of no worth, but not without meaning, many of the men thought. Wednesday's end was like that of the other days as the sun set behind the mountains and the searchers returned without Sarah.

"She will never be found," they agreed among themselves as they ate the food the women had prepared for them.

Despair attached itself to weariness. They had been beaten by circumstances and, shaking their heads sadly, they were ready to admit defeat. When the time came to leave, each man in his own way told John Whitcher he would not be back.

Pa nodded as he grasped the hands of his neighbors and thanked them for the help they had given. But when Ma saw them sling them their horns over their shoulders and pick up axes and guns, she ran to the ridge ahead of them and down the bridle path.

Standing in the middle of the path as they approached, she held out her hands to stop them. "Please, please," she implored, "don't leave us now."

The men stopped in their tracks and stared at her.

Ma opened her hands toward them as if to beg some kindness. "One more day, please."

Heads began to shake. "Useless," "Hopeless," were the words that passed among them.

"Kind friends, strangers, whoever you may be," Ma said in the gentling tone she had learned from Pa, "for the love you bear your own little ones, help us to find our child."

They could have brushed past her as if she had been a sapling gotten across their path, but no one moved.

Ma dropped her hands and waited.

The men looked away from her and at each other. Heads began to nod, a few words were murmured among them.

"We'll be back," one of them said gruffly.

Ma stepped aside to let them pass. "God bless you," she whispered as they went by her.

After the last man had disappeared from sight, Ma sank to her knees in a crumpled heap at the base of an oak tree. She prayed then, as she had not prayed before; she prayed as she knew her husband had been praying all along; and she remembered what he had said to her, "The Lord will find a way to help us all."

When she returned to the cabin she told her husband that the men had agreed to come back the next morning.

"It's too much to ask of them," Pa replied, but there was relief in his face. "They have their own work to do and they've given three days to us now. But one more — "

"Yes, one more, John." She slipped her hand into his as if even she was sure now, then she smiled up at him.

Into the clearing came the two Richardson boys and Little John, his hand on Ollie's shoulders. Ollie, hitched to the cart, was straining to draw its load.

"Ma thought you might need something to feed the folks tomorrow," the older boy said, "and she's coming up to be with you."

"Ollie wanted to help," Little John added.

Ma looked at the load and saw a bushel basket of beans, shelled and ready to be cooked. "That will feed a mighty lot of people," she said. "I'm thankful to have so much. You tell your mother so. And tell her I'll appreciate her coming up to help."

The Richardson boys turned and raced each other down the hill while Ollie drew the cart up close to the cauldron. Then Little John freed him from the harness and put his arms around the shaggy dog to thank him for his work. Over the bars to the pasture the foal lifted her head and whinnied. From the brook where she had been watering, the mare came cantering.

"Why is a white horse lucky, Ma?"

"I don't know, Little John, but it's always said to be."

"Will we find Sarah tomorrow?"

"Yes."

"You've been saying that every day."

"I'll go on saying it."

Pa smiled at Ma, proud of her, then he tousled Little John's red hair.

"John," Ma said impulsively, "let the three boys and me go along with you tomorrow."

Seeing the entreaty in his wife's face, the eagerness in his son's, Pa could not refuse. He nodded.

Little John made a glad sound, then ran off to tell his brothers.

◆ ◆ ◆

That Sunday night, when Sarah heard the rain pattering on the leaves high above her head, she knew that she must find some kind of shelter. It was dark in the forest and everything looked different. Peering around her, she saw something in the distance that looked like a cabin. She went toward it, not running now, but walking with careful steps and listening, listening. Reaching it she saw that it was a huge rock.

"It might be a kind of cabin," she said to herself, "a cabin made of stone instead of logs."

Keeping one hand on its rough side, she walked around it slowly, looking for a door. There was none, only a hollow place under one side. She leaned against the rock, thinking that when Pa came with his lantern she would show him the place that went down under the rock and ask him what it was.

"Pa!" she called again. "Ma!"

Far away there was the sound of a brook running over stones and falling in cascades. Berry Brook was near home. Pa would come for her soon.

She saw a dark shape moving among the trees and wondered what it was. Backing up hard against the boulder, she stood still and stared into the darkness as the shape came toward her.

"Ollie!" she exclaimed.

It looked like Ollie, even though he seemed so much bigger

than when he was back at the cabin. But then everything was different in the dim light — trees and rocks and — .

Maybe Ollie just looked bigger, Sarah thought. Maybe she, too, would look so much bigger that Ollie wouldn't know who she was and would walk right by her.

"Ollie," she called to him, hoping he would recognize her voice.

He came nearer and made a snuffling sound.

Sarah took a few steps forward to meet him. She tried to put her arms around him and hug him because he was there and found her. When she had to reach up to get her arms around his neck and bring his muzzle down to her face, she wondered if it really was Ollie. He not only looked bigger, he was bigger. He had a queer smell and his coat was rough and wet. Then all doubts were swept away as a warm red tongue began licking her cheeks, licking her arms and the scratches on them.

Finding the bunch of flowers Sarah was still clutching tightly in one hand, the inquisitive nose did not pass over them. Without wasting any time, strong white teeth began to crunch the flowers. Sarah was surprised, because she had not known Ollie to eat flowers before; but she was glad she had something he liked to reward him for coming to her.

When the flowers were all gone, she held her head close to his and stroked him with both hands. "Ollie," she whispered, "let me ride on your back when we go home."

Ollie bumped himself hard against Sarah. Puzzled, she soon realized she would have to do what he wanted her to do and that was take shelter under the rock. Nuzzling her toward the hollow place, he pushed her into it.

It was no more than a litter of leaves, but it was dry and so low that Sarah had to drop to her knees to keep from bumping her head. When Ollie followed her there was scarcely room for them both, but Ollie soon flattened his body against the wall, lying down on his side and taking up most of the space.

"Oh, Ollie, I'm so glad we've found each other." Sarah burrowed her head against him. "But you're wet and you smell!"

Reaching around her with a front paw. Ollie swatted her gently, drawing her into the curve made by his body. She fitted into the place as she had so often when they lay together by the hearth in Pa's cabin. From the shaggy body that encircled her small one came a deep humming sound.

"Ollie Oliverian, shall I tell you how you got your name?" At home Pa would be telling stories as Ma sat by the hearth with baby Henry on her lap and the others close by. It made Sarah feel near them if she did what they were doing.

The humming sound seemed to be Ollie's way of saying yes.

"When you were a tiny, tiny puppy, Ollie, no bigger than my hand," she began, and to make sure he understood she put her hand under his chin and rubbed him, "Pa brought you home to be a help to him. As soon as we played together, Pa knew what your name would be because he said you were as roistering as the Oliverian, so that's — how — you got your — name."

The words became slow-paced, farther and farther apart, for Sarah was beginning to feel sleepy. She was so warm and comfortable, and the sound that rumbled from deep within Ollie had the same effect as when Ma sang to them after she had tucked them all into bed at the end of the day. But Ma never let them get into bed until they had said their prayers. Sarah tried to move to find a way to her knees, but Ollie's hold tightened enough to make her realize that he didn't want her to move. She decided to pray as she was.

"Keep Pa and Ma safe, and bless — " Sleep overtook her before she could finish.

Later that night, when the rain ceased, the life of the forest came into its own. An owl called and another answered. There was a rush of wings as a sweep was made through the trees and a stifled cry when a small wanderer was caught in curved talons and soon devoured. A fox barked sharply, not the questing call to one of his kind, but a warning to all kinds to take cover. Distantly, then ever nearer, shouts could be heard and the blowing of horns; lanterns began to cast shadows. Voices became distinguishable as one man called and another answered.

Two men, approaching the big boulder from opposite sides, leaned against it to consult together. One stopped in mid-sentence to listen, then pointed to the hollow that went under the rock.

"Can you hear it?"

A steady drone of snoring reached their ears.

"That varmint's got himself a nice dry bed."

"I wouldn't like to be here when he wakes up."

"No more would I without my gun."

In another moment they had gone on, keeping enough space between them so each could see the glow of the other's lantern and respond to a call if it was made. After awhile, silence settled over the forest. Creatures kept to their lairs and men returned to their homes.

Sarah woke and rubbed her eyes, wondering where Betsey was and why it was so quiet in the cabin; then she remembered. She was alone now, but the place where Ollie had been lying was still warm. Bending her head to look out from the shelter, she saw Ollie disappearing in the distance, walking as if he knew where he was going.

"Ollie," she called, "Ollie, wait for me."

He did not heed her voice, nor did he turn around.

Surprised at his behavior, she soon told herself that Ollie had gone to get Pa and would bring him to where she was. She would stay there until they both came back. Hunching herself down again, she looked around her to see if there was any redding-up to do as Ma did first thing in the cabin, but there was scarcely enough light yet to see by. She curled up in the warm hollow and went to sleep again.

When she wakened, daylight had found its way into the shelter and Sarah, looking around her, could see that the bed of leaves needed to have nothing done to it, and the cocoons and lichens on the rock walls and ceiling looked as if they had always been there. She crawled out and found a patch of sunlight that felt as warm as Ollie's shaggy body. Then she looked around for something to eat.

There didn't seem to be anything, and she wondered if she should go back to the clearing where she had feasted on ripe strawberries; she decided to stay near the big rock so when Ollie came back with Pa, and maybe Ma, he would find her easily. She spied a hemlock with low sweeping branches and its tender tips of new growth offered her all she could eat for awhile. Satisfied, she sat down on the duff and played games with a collection of cones. When she tired of that, she built houses of twigs with clumps of moss for roofs.

In the far distance, and at different times during the day, she heard voices and dinner horns. Once she thought she heard her own name being called. Stopping her play to listen, she became quite sure that it was her name but it wasn't Pa's voice. She stood up with her back against a tree and shouted as loud as she could, "Here I am!"

Echoing through the woods, her own voice came back to her.

She tried again. "Pa! Ma!" and then with all her strength, "Ollie!"

Only an echo answered.

It gave her a queer feeling, as if there were someone else in the woods who was trying to be Sarah. She decided not to answer anymore. The sounds of calling and horns grew more distant; then they became so faint that she lost them altogether. It must have been somebody else who was being called. Not Sarah Whitcher.

◆ ◆ ◆

When it began to grow dusky, Sarah caught sight of Ollie loping along through the trees, alone as he had been yesterday, swinging his head from side to side. She ran to meet him. Putting her face to his nose, she reached up to get her arms around his neck.

"Oh, Ollie, where's Ma and Pa? I'm so hungry."

He pushed her with his head, and when they got to the boulder thumped her so she tumbled in among the dry leaves. There was something queer about the way he treated her, but she was so relieved to see him that she started laughing out

141

loud. Then when he followed her into the hollow, she pummeled him and pulled his hair, trying to find his tail.

Ollie was in no mood for a game. With one sweep of a forepaw he pulled her against his body, lay down, drew up his rear paws with his front paws tucked in close, and started licking her, vigorously, methodically.

"You're tickling me, Ollie!"

The embrace tightened, then the humming began.

Sarah's day had been long and lonely, but now that Ollie had come back to her she felt companioned.

"Shall I tell you a story, Ollie Oliverian, the way I did last night?"

The humming seemed to increase.

"Long, long ago, when Pa came to Pine Hill to build a cabin for us to live in, he sometimes got very hungry, for there weren't any chickens to lay eggs for him and no cow to give him milk. If a partridge flew by, Pa might catch it to roast over his fire, or a rabbit might come along to be made into a stew, but when nothing came by do you — know — what he did?" As drowsiness began to creep over her, Sarah pushed herself deeper into her furry haven; but she wanted to finish her story. "Do you — know — he went to sleep."

Her eyes closed. She brought her two hands together into a tight ball. She would do what Pa did when he was hungry and go to sleep.

The humming sound went on and on.

Wakened by Ollie's shift of position, Sarah saw dim light in the forest beyond the boulder. This morning she determined to follow Ollie when he crawled out into the open. She would follow him back to where Pa was and not wait for Pa to come to her. As soon as Ollie shook himself out of the bed of leaves, Sarah pursued him. She had to run to keep him in sight, as he loped away in the direction of the sound of the running brook. In the stillness of dawn, the sound made Sarah so aware of her thirst that she wondered if she could get to the water before her throat dried so that she would not be able to swallow. She didn't try to call his name again. It hadn't done any good. Catching up with Ollie at the brook, she waited for him to have his fill.

When he finished, he shook his head from side to side in a way she had never seen him do at the cabin, but she took it as answer to her earnest plea to wait for her until he went to Pa. She approached the sandy place and, kneeling a little upstream, put her face to the water. She drank and drank, then took time to wash her face and hands. When she stood up, Ollie was not waiting for her. He had gone away without her. She tried to find his tracks, but lost them in the underbrush, so she decided to return to the brook and wait for him there.

"Please come back soon, Ollie," she said aloud, not because there was much likelihood of his hearing her, but because the sound of her own voice was a change from the quietness around her, "and bring Ma and Pa with you."

Moving away from the sandy place to where the brook slipped over flat stones, she squatted down and started to build a dam. If her brothers had been there, Reuben would soon have found a way to make a mill wheel for the water to turn.

"Bring Joseph and Reuben and Little John back with you, Ollie," she called.

When she had finished her dam she was pleased with the small contained pool of water that made a washing place.

143

"And, Ollie, you might as well bring Betsey and baby Henry, for here is a good place for her to wash his things."

When hunger began to ache inside Sarah, she stopped playing and looked for something to eat. Cress was growing in the brook. She pulled some. It tasted good. She pulled up handfuls and ate it, but the empty feeling soon came back again.

Watching a bird approach the brook to drink, her eyes followed its motions as it wove among bordering grasses and disappeared from sight.

She followed it to where the grasses had stilled, then pushed them aside to see better.

At that moment the ground-nesting bird flew away with a chirping sound.

Sarah looked down and saw five speckled eggs in a small neat nest. She reached down and touched them. They were real, as real as any she had ever found for Pa in the barn, and they were warm. She put one up to her mouth, broke the shell against her teeth, and tipped her head back to let the contents run own her throat. One by one she ate them all and the hunger pain inside her went away.

She spent the whole day in her search for more food, and by the time Ollie found her at twilight she was no longer hungry but glad to see him, and filled with desire for a rough-and-tumble game. In the cabin, rolling on the floor together, she had often hung onto Ollie's tail and if he minded he never let her know. Now, in the woods, with dusk deepening around them, he acted very differently. He didn't seem to want to play the game. She crawled under him, but he swung around quickly and sat down. Laughing, she ran around to lean against him.

He promptly got up, and when she thought her hands would grasp his tail there was his nose in her face.

It was like a game of tag and hide-and-seek all in one. The more determined Sarah was to lay hands on a particular place, the more determined Ollie became to keep that place to himself. Whirling around and laughing, Sarah finally got her fingers where Ollie's tail should be, but the next moment a great paw swatted her down, knocked her over, and Ollie stood beside her growling.

"Ollie, what's happened to your tail? I don't think you've got one anymore."

The growling continued. Using one forepaw, then the other, Ollie rolled her over and over till she rolled into a depression in the ground. Getting his muzzle under her, he tossed her up in the air as Pa did a forkful of hay. She landed on the earth beside some rocks. Her head was whirling, and her body hurt as her stomach had earlier. For the first time she felt Ollie's nails. Dazed, she watched blood seeping from long scratches on her arms and legs.

In another moment Ollie was beside her, curving his body and drawing her into the curve, tightening his hold and moaning softly, then drawing his tongue over the scratches to clean them. She put her face into his shaggy hair and whispered to him that she would not try to play with his tail again.

"But please bring Ma and Pa back with you tomorrow, please, Ollie."

The moaning ceased, in time the humming started, and Sarah's fingers wound in and around the long, deep hair on Ollie's chest.

Sleep came too soon for any stories, and sleep was sound;

145

for the next morning when Sarah wakened, Ollie had gone. Peering around her with blinking eyes, she could not even see him disappearing in the distance as she had other mornings.

She lay still for a long time. Ollie had left her, and since he had not yet brought Pa to her, she decided that she would have to find Pa for herself. The brook was not far away, but she did not think it looked quite like Berry Brook that ran near the cabin. It was wider and the water ran deeper. She decided to follow it, thinking that perhaps it would join the brook she knew well, and then she could follow Berry Brook home.

Sarah crawled away from the rocks and stood up slowly. She smoothed her dress, which was now very dirty and torn in several places, then she found her way to the swiftly flowing stream.

There she washed her hands and scooped up mouthfuls of water that filled her so the ache within her eased. She washed her feet and debated washing her dress. It had a queer smell to it; it smelled like Ollie. Instead of washing she looked for food and took whatever offered itself — ferns, flower heads, the lichen that Pa called "poor man's bread." Occasionally something tasted so bitter that she spat it out.

The day was warm, even in the shade along the flowing water, and she felt sleepy. Turning away from the stream, she walked back again into the woods, slowly, stumbling often as if her bare feet had stones tied to them. She fell once, and when she picked herself up she stared at the new tear in her dress. She fell again, over a tree stump and against a rock. She did not pick herself up for a long time, not until it was well past noon.

When she resumed her journey, she saw in the distance

before her something that looked like shelter, so she started toward it. The sound of flowing water disappeared behind her and she became more aware of the sounds in the forest that were like distant voices and the blowing of horns. She had heard them so often that they seemed to belong to the forest. Sometimes near, sometimes far away, they were the wind moving in the trees, then moving off to lose itself in the sky.

Sarah stumbled on, rubbing her eyes with hands made into fists to try to see better. When she got to her goal, the shelter turned out to be the top of a pine tree blown from its butt in a recent storm. The needles were still green and there was the strong smell given off by oozing sap. Working her way in and under the branches, she wondered if Ollie would be able to find her; but she was too tired and hungry and hurting to think beyond that first wondering. Curling herself up with her head on her arms and her knees drawn close to her chin, she went to sleep. The sun had not yet set and the light had not yet become shadowy.

Ollie found her hours later. Lying down beside her, he curved his body to hers and began humming. Sarah opened her eyes a moment and loosed one hand to stroke him.

"Tomorrow, Ollie, please take me to Ma. Please, God," she whispered as she snuggled deeper into the warm comfort of Ollie's embrace.

◆ ◆ ◆

As soon as the sun came over the mountains on Thursday, promising a fourth day of fine weather, the search was resumed. A few of the men who lived at a great distance had to return to their own duties, but their places were taken by Ma and the three Whitcher boys. No doubt was in their minds, especially in Little John's, that this was the day Sarah would be found. When they started out, Little John was dragging behind him the cart with its pine-slab wheels.

"The ground is too rough, son," Pa said. "There's brush in many places, often stumps. When we go high there will be rocks. Much of the way there'll be no bridle path to follow."

"Could be she'll be tired and want to ride."

"It could be, and she will — on our shoulders."

"My shoulders, Pa?"

"She'll have her turn with each of us."

Little John trundled the cart over to Betsey and offered it to her for the day. She was pleased. It would make up to her for not going off with the rest of the family. Ma had put her in charge, not only of baby Henry but of the cabin.

"You're needed here, Betsey, and Ollie will stay by to help you."

"Yes, Ma."

Mrs. Patch and Mrs. Richardson, each one with a small child, had come to the cabin to prepare food and have all in readiness for the searchers' return. Betsey stood beside them. They watched the party go off, dividing at the ridge as they had other days into groups taking different directions. Faint and far away grew the sound of the horns, but the sound was always in the air like a low moaning wind.

"I'd like to be with them," Mrs. Patch said.

Mrs. Richardson agreed. "But somebody's got to keep the fire and see to the food."

Betsey tugged at Mrs. Patch's skirt. "Once upon a time I found a four-leaf clover in the pasture," she confided. "If they'd let me go along, I could find my sister." She lifted her head. "I'm sure I could."

"Bless you, child, but it would take more than four-leaf clover eyes to find her." She put her arms around the little girl, sensing her need for comfort, then she released her with a sturdy shove. "Let's get to our work, for we've all got something to do. Betsey, fetch buckets so we can have the water we need, then take care of those children so no one of them will get too near the fire. That toddler of mine is apt to go most anywhere if you don't keep an eye on him."

Betsey got the buckets, then she tied Ollie to the cart, piled the two visiting children in with baby Henry and went off to a shady place by the pasture wall. She had a fund of stories to tell and some songs to sing. When the little ones began to get restless, Ollie helped to keep them entertained. When he swung his tail, the children played with it as if it were a rope; when he lowered his body, they climbed on his back.

The two women sat on the bench by the cabin, fingering through the bushel of beans for bits of shell or stem. When the water in the cauldron over the fire came to a good rolling boil, they tipped the beans into it, added a huge hunk of salt pork and a dozen or more onions.

"That'll be a tasty mess five hours from now," Mrs. Patch said as she watched the big brown bubbles form slowly and then break away.

"There may be those without the heart to eat."

"I hope not, I'd like to think that success will be theirs today and they'll return with appetites worthy of all we've got in this cauldron."

"My man says that child couldn't have survived one night

in the forest, leastways four. The days may be warm enough but the nights can still chill the marrow in your bones. And what did she have on but a little thin cotton dress!"

Mrs. Patch made no comment.

"There isn't any one of all those men out scouring the mountains day after day who believes she'll be found. Alive, that is."

"Yes, there is," Mrs. Patch was quick in her reply, "John Whitcher."

"Well, he's her father!"

When it was almost noon, the children were summoned and fed. There was cold mush remaining from the morning meal and plenty of milk. The aroma from the cauldron was beginning to penetrate the air, and Betsey sniffed excitedly.

"Will we be having beans, too?"

"Yes, child, there's enough to feed forty men, but they won't all want to eat hearty."

When Mrs. Richardson started to gather the children up to get them into the cabin for a rest, she included Betsey, who objected. "Ma put me in charge. I'm staying here with you."

"So she did, but you'll do better later on, when we'll be needing your help, if you have a mite of rest now. Come along. Neither one of us will move from this bench by the cabin until you're all awake again. It won't be any time after that before the men will be back."

"With Sarah."

It was not a question, so Mrs. Richardson did not answer.

Soon the children were tucked under a quilt in the big bed. Henry fitted into the space beside Betsey's slight body, as he did against his mother's more ample one, so the Patch baby could have the use of the cradle. Ollie stretched out across the doorway.

"They'll be quiet for an hour or more."

"Then they'll be wanting something to eat."

"They can have a taste of the pottage."

The two women, sitting on the bench and leaning back against the rough wall of the cabin, took what rest they could. The sound of horns still echoed through the forest, and from hill to mountain, but so accustomed had they become to it that it was no longer even heard. Another sound caused Mrs. Patch to open her eyes drowsily. Nailed boots were striking on stones in the path. Was it another man come to join the search? Or one of the searchers returning with news?

A few moments later a young man came down the ridge and into the clearing. Neither woman had to look twice to see that he was a stranger. A leather sack over his shoulder proclaimed him to be a wayfarer.

"He may be wanting direction," Mrs. Richardson whispered.

"He's a bean pole of a man," Mrs. Patch added, "and he looks mile-worn."

They remained quiet as he came across the clearing to stand in front of them.

"I've come from Plymouth," he said. His words were weary, uttered through parched lips.

"Afoot? That's close to thirty miles."

He nodded.

"Where are you bound?"

"To find the child."

"The child!" Both women gasped.

"Give me some food and water, for I'm faint with hunger; then show me the bridle path to the north."

"You've come to find *Sarah?*" Mrs. Richardson asked.

"If that's her name."

"I hope you know these mountains."

He shook his head. "I've never been this far north before."

The two women exchanged glances, then Mrs. Richardson spoke again, and tartly. "When forty men who know these mountains as well as they know their own clearings can't find Sarah Whitcher, how is it you think you can?"

"Please, kind ladies, I've walked from Plymouth, I've not stopped for rest or food along the way. Give me something to eat."

"'Tis a mess of beans cooking for the men's supper," Mrs. Patch said as she fetched a bowl, then ladeled a generous portion into it. "This will put strength into you. Sit down now and eat."

Mrs. Richardson handed the young man a noggin of water. "It's the last day for the search."

He took it and bowed slightly to each woman. "My name is Heath," he said, "and I thank you kindly." Shifting the leather sack from his shoulders, he leaned it against the cabin, then sat down on the bench. The noggin of water was drained and refilled before he turned himself to the bowl of bean pottage.

"I doubt that they'll find Sarah now," Mrs. Richardson shook her head sadly, "even her little body or any tatters of her clothes, but there'll be a good meal waiting for them all when they get back."

"I shall find her," Mr. Heath said quietly.

"You!"

When he had finished he set the bowl down on the bench, shook his head at the offer of more, and said, "Last night, when I walked into the inn at Plymouth, I heard talk of a lost child. When I went to bed I dreamed of finding her."

"A dream!" Mrs. Richardson exclaimed, then she burst out laughing. "It will take more than a dream to find Sarah now."

Unperturbed by her laughter and beginning to look refreshed from rest and food, Mr. Heath went on. "It was no ordinary dream. It woke me from my sleep, not once but three times."

"And in it you *saw* Sarah?" Mrs. Patch asked eagerly.

"I did. She was safe in a shelter made by boughs and she was guarded by a bear. It was cubbing her as if it were her mother. Her mother," he repeated.

Mrs. Richardson caught her breath. "Was she alive or dead?"

"The dream only showed her in the place where she would be found."

"Pray God that you dream true!"

"And the dream woke you three times?" Mrs. Patch wanted to return to the story.

"Yes. Each time I saw more clearly, the way a bird sees the country above which it flies." Mr. Heath made a wide sweep with one of his long arms. "I saw this cabin and the path leading to it. I saw a bridle path that went into the woods in a northerly direction. I saw the place where boughs had fallen and under them I saw the child."

"When did you leave Plymouth?"

"It must have been near midnight."

"And you followed the course of the Baker River?"

"Then you came up Berry Brook?"

"I did not know the names."

At that moment Betsey, wakened by the sound of voices came to stand in the doorway, rubbing the sleep from her eyes.

Mr. Heath stared at her, leaning forward he looked more closely, then he gave a slight shake of his head.

"Was this the child you saw?" Mrs. Richardson asked.

"No, but there is a resemblance. I thought, almost — no, no," he shook his head vigorously, "the child I saw had red hair."

Betsey, wide awake now, went up to Mr. Heath. "Are you going to find my little sister?"

He nodded and bent over to tighten the laces on his boots. "If someone will put me on the bridle path to the north."

Joseph Patch came out of the woods and approached the cabin. His gun was carried in his right hand, a dinner horn damp from much blowing hung over one shoulder.

"Husband!" his wife cried as she ran toward him. "This young man has come to find Sarah."

"No one can. Now."

"Oh, but he has had a wonderful dream. He knows where she is. He will show you."

Joseph Patch shook his head wearily.

Taking hold of his arm, she started toward the cabin with him. Her tone changed from one of joyous excitement to something more serious. "I think that you must heed him, husband."

Joseph Patch looked long and hard at the stranger on the bench by the cabin, as if in this last moment he might be willing to believe anything. "So?"

Mr. Heath rose and went up to him. "Can you show me the place where a bridle path going north crosses a good-sized brook?"

"That will be the Oliverian. We call it a river. I know the place."

Speaking slowly to give meaning to his words, Mr. Heath explained, "A few rods southeast of the crossing there is a pine top lying on the ground. Under it is where the child will be found."

"That crossing is close to an hour's walk from here."

"No matter."

Too tired to question further, too tired even to doubt, Joseph Patch nodded to his wife, then turned back to face the forest. "I'll show you where it is."

Without another word, Mr. Heath fell into step beside him, and the two men went off toward the ridge, arms swinging, long legs loose in their stride.

"Now I know it's a lucky thing to have two white horses," Betsey chirped.

In the pasture the mare was standing under the shade of a maple tree, her tail flicking; nearby and flat on the ground, still as a fallen leaf, the foal was asleep.

"Strange things do happen," Mrs. Richardson admitted. "Seems as if you almost have to believe a man when he's as sure of himself as that young man is."

Mrs. Patch, stirring the beans in the cauldron, smiled but would not trust herself to speak. When she went into the cabin to see to the children, Betsey followed her happily.

◆ ◆ ◆

The two men said little as they walked up and over the ridge, then took the bridle path to the north. Only once did they stop. That was where the path crossed the Oliverian. It was a shallow place and both men knelt to drink and refresh themselves.

On the far side of the brook, Joseph Patch said, "Now you're the one to lead."

"And I will," Heath replied. Walking forward a few steps, he hesitated for a moment, then turned to the left and plunged into some low-growing brush.

"There's no way there. You'd best come back."

"It's my way and it's the way I'm going."

Drawn by the young man's sureness and his own desire not to lose another person, Patch followed. "How far are you going in this?"

"A few rods. Bear to the southeast and hold to your bearings. Keep within sound of my voice."

Ahead of him Heath saw a massive pine, its top blown off in a recent gale, its gaping trunk open like a wound to the sky. Eagerly he thrust his way to where the blown top lay and saw the child just as he had seen her in the dream, asleep. But alone. He paused until Joseph Patch came up beside him and both stood gazing at little Sarah Whitcher, lost and now found. Her face was stained, her dress was torn, her arms and legs were scratched; but her lips were parted slightly and her chest rose and fell with her breathing.

"You'll be the one to wake her," Heath said quietly. "Likely she knows your face, and I'd be a stranger to her."

"She knows me most as well as any of my own little ones." Patch handed his gun to Heath. "When I have her close folded in my arms, fire. The signal is three shots in quick succession; wait till the count of five, then fire another two in rapid succession: found alive."

Patch reached in through the tangle of branches where Sarah lay asleep. He put his arms under her and gently lifted her up.

Sarah opened her eyes. "I want my mother," she murmured. Putting her head against the friendly shoulder, she whispered, "Carry me home to my mother."

Heath fired the three shots, waited the required time, then fired the two that completed the story. Almost like an echo, the mountain world came alive with sound — shots were fired, dinner horns were blown, people could be heard shouting.

The two men walked back through the brush to the bridle path at the crossing of the Oliverian, and while they waited Joseph Patch gave Sarah a drink of the clear cold water. Soon others began to gather around them, coming up the path, down the path, and out of the woods, all eager for a sight of the child.

"It's true! The little one has been found!"

"She's alive! God be praised."

Men who had secretly disbelieved she would ever be found were put to understand how it had come about. They turned from her to the young man for explanation. Over and over he repeated the words, "I saw her in a dream. Mr. Patch led me to the place."

Ashamed now of his first unwillingness, Joseph Patch shook his head. "He would have found her without me. He was that sure."

When the Whitchers arrived, panting from their long run over rough ground, a shout went up from the crowd. Everyone spoke at once about the young man and his dream, pointing to him, gesturing. They fell back to make way for Ma and Pa in their midst, then Joseph Patch stepped forward to place Sarah in her mother's arms.

"Sarah! Sarah, our little Sarah!" Ma cried. Whatever words might have followed were lost in the tears of joy that overcame her.

Then Sarah saw her father and reached toward him.

He swung her up in his arms and held her above his head while men cheered and the three boys danced around him shouting, "Sarah's been found! Our sister's been found!" Pa soon put her back in Ma's arms.

The stranger in the crowd was the young man standing near Joseph Patch. Pa went up to him and grasped one hand in both of his. Pa's pale blue eyes looked into the young man's, and words he might never be able to say were in his long glance. Like the dropping of a wind, silence settled through the crowd. Only the Oliverian, rushing over its rocky bed on its way to the valley, could be heard.

"I didn't know what the Lord was going to do nor how He'd do it," John Whitcher said, "but I knew He'd do something. And He did."

Silence again, and the river running through it; silence broken by a child's voice saying, "He made everything come out right."

"Amen," someone on the edge of the crowd murmured. It was repeated until everyone had said it not once but many times; repeated until it became a great rolling sound that wrapped them all up in wonder at what had happened.

Then they started down the bridle path, led by the Whitcher family.

"Want to walk," Sarah struggled in her mother's arms, "want to walk with the people."

"Not until your brothers have had a chance to give you a

ride," Pa said as he lifted her free, then set her first on Little John's shoulders. After a few rods along the path he lifted her up again and placed her on Reuben's, and finally on Joseph's.

"Where's Ollie?"

"Waiting for you at home."

It took almost an hour to reach the cabin, but the news went ahead. The signal, heard and understood by the women, set them to speeding up preparations for the meal. When the three boys came running into the clearing with the full story, the women listened eagerly. Nothing would do for them then but to leave the boys in charge of the fire and the pottage and go up the path to see for themselves and welcome the little girl.

Mr. Heath walked behind Ma and Pa, enjoying the sight of Sarah's red head bobbing above her father as she rode on his shoulders. She had accepted a piece of bread someone put in her hands but soon discovered that a few bites were all she wanted. Too happy to try to swallow and excited by all the attention she was getting, Sarah offered the bread to Mr. Heath, who took it from her with a word of thanks.

Everyone wanted to touch her. Everyone wanted to ask her about her time in the forest.

"Weren't you lonely?"

"Weren't you frightened?"

Over and over the same questions were asked as more searchers came out of the woods and caught up with the crowd going down the path. To them all Sarah had the same answer. "Ollie came to me every night and kept me warm."

When she first said it, Pa had looked sharply at Ma. Ollie spent the nights outside to guard the stock, but had he gone to the forest to be with Sarah he would have brought her home as he sometimes did a lamb or a calf that had strayed. Ma knew what Pa meant.

Now, perched on Pa's broad shoulders, Sarah began to sing to herself about her shaggy dog, her big black dog whose name was Ollie Oliverian and whose coat was warmer than any blanket.

When they got within sight of the cabin and she spied Ollie in the doorway with Betsey beside him, she begged Pa to put her down. Standing unsteadily for a moment, then tottering as she ran, Sarah went toward the cabin calling Ollie's name.

He made no move except to wag his tail uncertainly.

Just before Sarah reached him she stopped short. "You've grown so small, Ollie? What's happened to you?'

He took a step toward her, then halted. Ears laid back, he stretched his neck out until his nose nearly touched her, sniffing, sniffing. His hackles rose. A low growl vibrated in his throat.

Sarah moved quickly and threw her arms around him, longing for nothing so much as to curl up against his warm body. "Sing to me, Ollie, the way you used to sing to me in the woods."

Pa and Ma drew near. Ollie looked up at them with questioning. His tail was poised, his ears were laid back, his whole attention was diverted by the strong musk smell that had always meant just one thing to him

"Take care of her, Ollie," Pa said.

Ollie crumpled to the earth and Sarah fitted herself against his body.

"Let her rest," Ma said. "It'll be time enough to wash and dress her when we've all had something to eat."

"She's tired from the excitement," Mrs. Patch agreed, while Mrs. Richardson stared at the little girl as if she could not see enough of her.

The young man went toward the bench to pick up his leather sack. He slung it over his shoulder and started to make his way through the crowd that had gathered around the fire.

"You'll stay, won't you, Mr. Heath, and have some food with us?" Ma's voice was as gay as birdsong.

"Thank you, ma'am, but I've already had a good share. I'd best be going on my way." He smiled at her, then turned to Pa.

The two men clasped hands again.

Ma and Pa watched him as he went up to the ridge. At the top he turned and waved to them. They raised their hands and waved to him before he went from their sight.

Mrs. Patch and Mrs. Richardson had been filling bowls from the cauldron, but before anyone dipped a spoon into the pottage, there was a blessing to be said and they waited for Pa to say it. He led them in singing "Old Hundred."

"Praise God from whom all blessings flow;
Praise Him, all creatures here below — "

Men, women, children sang as they had never sung before, and Pa's voice soared above them all.

As young Mr. Heath went down the bridle path, the sound of singing went with him.

❧ Author Biographies ❧

Lloyd Alexander (1924-   ) is best known for his creation of the Prydain series, a five-book set based on the collection of Welsh myths known as the Mabinogion. The books feature the adventures of Taran, a boy who, at the outset of the first book, *The Book of Three*, is an Assistant Pig-Keeper. By the final book, *The High King*, he has come to terms with his identity and has matured into a just leader who, tempered by his experiences, begins to rebuild his home-land, which was devastated by war. *The High King* won the 1969 Newbery Medal, a fitting end to one of the most popular children's fantasy series ever written.

Alexander has written more than twenty-five books for children and young adults, including the acclaimed **Westover** trilogy, and many novels for adults. He is a member of the Editorial Advisory Board for the children's magazine **Cricket**. Born in Philadelphia, Pennsylvania, he studied at West Chester State College and Lafayette College in Pennsylvania before attending the University of Paris in 1946. He also served in the United States Army Combat Intelligence and Counter-Intelligence Corps during the latter half of World War II. Before turning to writing, he was a cartoonist, translator, layout artist, copywriter, and editor of an industrial magazine. His awards beside the Newbery are too numerous to list here, but include sever-al "Best Book of the Year" awards, the National Book Award, and other awards from around the world. Alexander and his wife, Janine, whom he met in France, currently live in Drexel Hills, Pennsylvania.

◆   ◆   ◆

Betsy Byars (1928-   ) is the pseudonym of **Betsy Cromer**, who has written literally dozens of young adult novels dealing with the ordinary and not-so-ordinary trials of children and teenagers growing up in the modern age. Her 1971 Newbery Medal-winning book *Summer of the Swans* deals with a teenage girl, Sara, and her struggle to cope with adolescence, sibling rivalry with her older sister, family troubles, and the responsibility of dealing with her mentally impaired younger brother, Charlie. Her adventures during the sum-mer begin with a group of swans that appear on the lake near her family's West Virginia home. Ultimately, Sara matures in a realistic way that many young adult readers identify with.

Byars was born in Charlotte, North Carolina, and attended school at Furman University in South Carolina. She then went to Queens College in Charlotte, where she attained a B.A. in English in 1950. She began writing in the mid-1960s and has published more than forty-nine books for children. Several of her novels were made into episodes of the long-running series *The ABC Afterschool Special*, including *Summer of the Swans*, *The Night Swimmers*, *The 18th Emergency*, and *The Winged Colt of Casa Mia*.

She has won too many awards to count, including the *New York Times* Outstanding Book of the Year for *The Winged Colt of Casa Mia*, and ten of her books have been chosen as America's Book of the Year by the Child Study Association. She lives in Clemson, South Carolina, with her husband, Ed, a college professor. They have four children and five grandchildren.

◆ ◆ ◆

Elizabeth Coatsworth (1893-1986) was an author whose primary interest was the ever-changing America she grew up in. She wrote about a diverse range of subjects, from the Vikings when they invaded Ireland in *The Wanderers* to the legendary inhabitants of the Norway's fjords and mountains in *Troll Weather*. She always returned, however, to the vast American landscape for inspiration. Although her 1931 Newbery-winning story *The Cat Who Went to Heaven* is set in medieval Japan, the United States, especially the New England coastline, is the setting for most of her books.

Many critics have lauded the tetralogy of her New England novels, loosely called "The Incredible Tales" — which consist of *Silky, The Enchanted*, *Mountain Bride*, and *The White Room* — as her best work, with their lyric descriptions of the deep forests of the New England countryside. The people and cultures of the region are warmly brought to life in stories that combine New Englanders' common sense with the feeling of entering a modern legend.

Born in Buffalo, New York, Coatsworth was educated at Los Robles School in Pasadena, California. Then she came back to the Northeast to study at Buffalo Seminary and Vassar College in

Poughkeepsie, New York, where she received her B.A., and Columbia University, where she received her M.A. She married noted author Henry Beston in 1929 and raised two daughters with him until his death in 1968.

She was the author of over one hundred books of poetry, short stories, and novels for both children and adults.

◆ ◆ ◆

Christopher Paul Curtis (1954-   ) has had remarkable success with his first two books. His debut young adult novel, *The Watsons Go to Birmingham — 1963*, the story of an African-American family's trip south in the 1960s, was named both a 1996 Newbery Honor Book and a Coretta Scott King Honor Book, the award for an African-American writer making an inspirational and educational contribution to children's literature. His second book, *Bud, Not Buddy*, tells the touching story of a ten-year-old African-American boy who lives in foster homes during the Depression and eventually runs away to find his father. His second book topped his first book, winning both the Newbery Medal and the Coretta Scott King Award for 2000. Curtis has garnered not only wide critical acclaim but a devoted following among diverse audiences. His books are among the few in young adult fiction to present African-American role models.

What is truly amazing is that he began writing while working full-time at the Fisher Body plant in Flint, Michigan, the city where he was born and the site of his books. He went to work at the plant after completing high school and says that he hated working there, but writing took his mind off it. He also went back to school, studying political science at the University of Michigan. Curtis and his wife, Kaysandra, a nurse, currently live in Windsor, Ontario, Canada, with their son and daughter. He enjoys visiting schools and talking to children about writing.

◆ ◆ ◆

Will James (1892-1942) was the cowboy pseudonym for Joseph Ernest Nepthtali Dufault, the author of several collections of cowboy stories, which, along with his western adult novels, made up the majority of his fiction output.

A cowboy and rodeo rider himself, James brought the American West alive in his stories, writing in the idiosyncratic dialect of the range cowboy. His depiction of the relationship between the cowboy and his horse, recreated memorably in the Newbery Medal-winning book *Smoky, the Cowhorse*, published in 1926, resurrected an image of the West that was fast dying out. A large part of what made his books so absorbing were his own illustrations, featuring well-muscled horses in powerful, realistic action scenes.

Unfortunately, his past caught up with him. He served a prison sentence for cattle rustling in 1915 before turning to writing, and later, after he wrote his autobiography, it was discovered by outside authenticators that his written life was almost entirely made up, created out of the cowboy illusions that he wrote, ironically, with such realism.

◆ ◆ ◆

Lois Lenski (1893-1974) is known primarily for her series of middle-school books detailing the lives of everyday American families. Volumes such as *Cotton in My Sack*, *Shoo-Fly Girl*, and *San Francisco Boy*, respectively, detail the fictional lives of a Southern sharecropper girl, a Pennsylvania Amish girl, and a Chinese-American boy living in San Francisco. These books are made all the more real by the author's exhaustive research into the lives of these various regional groups of people, often including visits to see their day-to-day activities in person.

Born in Springfield, Ohio, she earned a B.S. in education from Ohio State University, then went on to study at the Art Students' League in New York and the prestigious Westminster School of Art in London. Right after school, she married the artist Arthur Covey and raised their son and two stepchildren with him until his death in 1960. Her artwork garnered her several single artist shows, notably a display of oil paintings in the Weyhe Gallery and a watercolors show in the Ferargils Gallery, both in New York. She also was included in group art shows at the Pennsylvania Water Color Show and the New York Water Color Show.

During her lifetime, she wrote more than one hundred books of stories, poetry, and plays, the majority of them illustrated by her as well. Her autobiography, *Journey into Childhood*, was finished two years before her death.

◆ ◆ ◆

Elizabeth Yates (1905-   ) is the pseudonym for **Elizabeth Yates McGreal**, who researched and turned the real-life story of a slave in colonial America and his fight to be free into the book *Amos Fortune, Free Man*, winner of the 1951 Newbery Medal. Besides writing about Amos Fortune, Yates has chronicled the lives of other people who have challenged society, such as Dorothy Canfield Fisher, David Livingstone, and Prudence Crandall, who, in Connecticut in 1833, began the first school to accept European and African-American children on an equal basis.

Courageous characters populate Yates's fiction as well. In *Carolina's Courage*, a young girl's fearlessness and spirit are put to the test when she befriends a little Native American girl. The gifts the two exchange, Carolina's beautiful porcelain doll for the other girl's buffalo hide one, inadvertently save her family from hostile Native Americans.

Writing is a subject dear to Yates's heart, as evidenced by her willingness to speak to school groups in her area, even when she was well into her eighties. She has also written the book *Someday You'll Write*, a primer for children that emphasizes patience, hard work, and perseverance as requirements for success.

Born in Buffalo, New York, Yates married William McGreal, and the two lived in England for a number of years before settling on a New Hampshire farm in 1939. Yates has written and lectured about writing for decades, teaching at various colleges such as the Universities of Connecticut, New Hampshire, and Indiana. She has also instructed at various Christian Writers and Editors conferences and is a Trustee of the Peterborough Town Library in New Hampshire. She has received several honorary degrees, most notably literary degrees from Aurora University, Ripon College, the University of New Hampshire, and Rivier College.

❧ Newbery Award-Winning Books ❧

2000
WINNER:
Bud, Not Buddy by Christopher Paul Curtis

HONOR BOOKS:
Getting Near to Baby by Audrey Couloumbis

Our Only May Amelia by Jennifer L. Holm

26 Fairmount Avenue by Tomie dePaola

1999
WINNER:
Holes by Louis Sachar

HONOR BOOK:
A Long Way from Chicago by Richard Peck

1998
WINNER:
Out of the Dust by Karen Hesse

HONOR BOOKS:
Ella Enchanted by Gail Carson Levine

Lily's Crossing by Patricia Reilly Giff

Wringer by Jerry Spinelli

1997
WINNER:
The View from Saturday by E.L. Konigsburg

HONOR BOOKS:
Belle Prater's Boy by Ruth White

A Girl Named Disaster by Nancy Farmer

Moorchild by Eloise McGraw

The Thief by Megan Whalen Turner

1996
WINNER:
The Midwife's Apprentice by Karen Cushman

HONOR BOOKS:
The Great Fire by Jim Murphy

The Watsons Go to Birmingham — 1963 by Christopher Paul Curtis

What Jamie Saw by Carolyn Coman

Yolanda's Genius by Carol Fenner

1995
WINNER:
Walk Two Moons by Sharon Creech

HONOR BOOKS:
Catherine, Called Birdy by Karen Cushman

The Ear, the Eye, and the Arm by Nancy Farmer

1994
WINNER:
The Giver by Lois Lowry

HONOR BOOKS:
Crazy Lady by Jane Leslie Conly

Dragon's Gate by Laurence Yep

Eleanor Roosevelt: A Life of Discovery by Russell Freedman

1993
WINNER:
Missing May by Cynthia Rylant

HONOR BOOKS:
The Dark-thirty: Southern Tales of the Supernatural by Patricia McKissack

Somewhere in the Darkness by Walter Dean Myers

What Hearts by Bruce Brooks

1992
WINNER:
Shiloh by Phyllis Reynolds Naylor

HONOR BOOKS:
Nothing But the Truth:
A Documentary Novel
by Avi

The Wright Brothers: How They
Invented the Airplane
by Russell Freedman

1991

WINNER:
Maniac Magee by Jerry Spinelli

HONOR BOOK:
The True Confessions of
Charlotte Doyle
by Avi

1990

WINNER:
Number the Stars by Lois Lowry

HONOR BOOKS:
Afternoon of the Elves
by Janet Taylor Lisle

Shabanu Daughter
of the Wind
by Suzanne Fisher Staples

The Winter Room by Gary Paulsen

1989

WINNER:
Joyful Noise: Poems for Two Voices
by Paul Fleischman

HONOR BOOKS:
In the Beginning: Creation Stories
from around the World
by Virginia Hamilton

Scorpions by Walter Dean Myers

1988

WINNER:
Lincoln: A Photobiography
by Russell Freedman

HONOR BOOKS:
After the Rain
by Norma Fox Mazer

Hatchet by Gary Paulsen

1987

WINNER:
The Whipping Boy by Sid Fleischman

HONOR BOOKS:
A Fine White Dust by Cynthia Rylant

On My Honor by Marion Dane Bauer

Volcano: The Eruption and
Healing of Mount St. Helens
by Patricia Lauber

1986

WINNER:
Sarah, Plain and Tall
by Patricia MacLachlan

HONOR BOOKS:
Commodore Perry in the
Land of the Shogun
by Rhonda Blumberg

Dogsong by Gary Paulsen

1985

WINNER:
The Hero and the Crown
by Robin McKinley

HONOR BOOKS:
Like Jake and Me by Mavis Jukes

The Moves Make the Man
by Bruce Brooks

One-Eyed Cat by Paula Fox

1984

WINNER:
Dear Mr. Henshaw by Beverly Cleary

HONOR BOOKS:
The Sign of the Beaver
by Elizabeth George Speare

A Solitary Blue by Cynthia Voigt

Sugaring Time by Kathryn Lasky

The Wish Giver: Three
Tales of Coven Tree
by Bill Brittain

1983

WINNER:
Dicey's Song by Cynthia Voigt

HONOR BOOKS:
The Blue Sword by Robin McKinley
Doctor DeSoto by William Steig
Graven Images by Paul Fleischman
Homesick: My Own Story by Jean Fritz
Sweet Whispers, Brother Rush
by Virginia Hamilton

1982

WINNER:
A Visit to William Blake's Inn:
Poems for Innocent and
Experienced Travelers
by Nancy Willard

HONOR BOOKS:
Ramona Quimby, Age 8
by Beverly Cleary

Upon the Head of the Goat: A
Childhood in Hungary 1939-1944
by Aranka Siegal

1981

WINNER:
Jacob Have I Loved
by Katherine Paterson

HONOR BOOKS:
The Fledgling by Jane Langton
A Ring of Endless Light
by Madeleine L'Engle

1980

WINNER:
A Gathering of Days: A New England
Girl's Journal, 1830-1832
by Joan W. Blos

HONOR BOOK:
The Road from Home: The
Story of an Armenian Girl
by David Kherdian

1979

WINNER:
The Westing Game by Ellen Raskin

HONOR BOOK:
The Great Gilly Hopkins
by Katherine Paterson

1978

WINNER:
Bridge to Terabithia
by Katherine Paterson

HONOR BOOKS:
Anpao: An American Indian Odyssey
by Jamake Highwater
Ramona and Her Father
by Beverly Cleary

1977

WINNER:
Roll of Thunder, Hear My Cry
by Mildred D. Taylor

HONOR BOOKS:
Abel's Island by William Steig
A String in the Harp by Nancy Bond

1976

WINNER:
The Grey King by Susan Cooper

HONOR BOOKS:
Dragonwings by Laurence Yep
The Hundred Penny Box
by Sharon Bell Mathis

1975

WINNER:
M.C. Higgins, the Great
by Virginia Hamilton

HONOR BOOKS:
Figgs & Phantoms by Ellen Raskin
My Brother Sam Is Dead
by James Lincoln Collier
and Christopher Collier

The Perilous Gard
by Elizabeth Marie Pope

Philip Hall Likes Me, I Reckon Maybe
by Bette Greene

1974

WINNER:
The Slave Dancer by Paula Fox

HONOR BOOK:
The Dark Is Rising by Susan Cooper

1973

WINNER:
Julie of the Wolves
by Jean Craighead George

HONOR BOOKS:
Frog and Toad Together
by Arnold Lobel
The Upstairs Room by Johanna Reiss
The Witches of Worm
by Zilpha Keatley Snyder

1972

WINNER:
Mrs. Frisby and the Rats of NIMH
by Robert C. O'Brien

HONOR BOOKS:
Annie and the Old One
by Miska Miles
The Headless Cupid
by Zilpha Keatley Snyder
Incident at Hawk's Hill
by Allan W. Eckert
The Planet of Junior Brown
by Virginia Hamilton
The Tombs of Atuan
by Ursula K. Le Guin

1971

WINNER:
Summer of the Swans by Betsy Byars

HONOR BOOKS:
Enchantress from the Stars
by Sylvia Louise Engdahl
Knee Knock Rise by Natalie Babbitt
Sing Down the Moon by Scott O'Dell

1970

WINNER:
Sounder by William H. Armstrong

HONOR BOOKS:
Journey Outside by Mary Q. Steele
*The Many Ways of Seeing: An
Introduction to the Pleasures of Art*
by Janet Gaylord Moore
Our Eddie by Sulamith Ish-Kishor

1969

WINNER:
The High King by Lloyd Alexander

HONOR BOOKS:
To Be a Slave by Julius Lester
*When Shlemiel Went to Warsaw
and Other Stories*
by Isaac Bashevis Singer

1968

WINNER:
*From the Mixed-Up Files of
Mrs. Basil E. Frankweiler*
by E.L. Konigsburg

HONOR BOOKS:
The Black Pearl
by Scott O'Dell
The Egypt Game
by Zilpha Keatley Snyder
The Fearsome Inn
by Isaac Bashevis Singer
*Jennifer, Hecate, Macbeth, William
McKinley, and Me, Elizabeth*
by E.L. Konigsburg

1967

WINNER:
Up a Road Slowly by Irene Hunt

HONOR BOOKS:
The Jazz Man by Mary Hays Weik
The King's Fifth by Scott O'Dell
*Zlateh the Goat and
Other Stories*
by Isaac Bashevis Singer

1966

WINNER:
I, Juan de Pareja
by Elizabeth Borton de Trevino

HONOR BOOKS:
The Animal Family
by Randall Jarrell
The Black Cauldron
by Lloyd Alexander
The Noonday Friends by Mary Stolz

1965

WINNER:
Shadow of a Bull
by Maia Wojciechowska

HONOR BOOK:
Across Five Aprils by Irene Hunt

1964

WINNER:
It's Like This, Cat by Emily Neville

HONOR BOOKS:
The Loner by Ester Wier
Rascal: A Memoir of a Better Era
by Sterling North

1963

WINNER:
A Wrinkle in Time
by Madeleine L'Engle

HONOR BOOKS:
Men of Athens by Olivia Coolidge
*Thistle and Thyme: Tales and
Legends from Scotland*
by Sorche Nic Leodhas

1962

WINNER:
The Bronze Bow
by Elizabeth George Speare

HONOR BOOKS:
Belling the Tiger by Mary Stolz
Frontier Living by Edwin Tunis
The Golden Goblet
by Eloise Jarvis McGraw

1961

WINNER:
Island of the Blue Dolphins
by Scott O'Dell

HONOR BOOKS:
*America Moves Forward:
A History for Peter*
by Gerald W. Johnson
The Cricket in Times Square
by George Selden
Old Ramon by Jack Schaefer

1960

WINNER:
Onion John by Joseph Krumgold

HONOR BOOKS:
*American Is Born:
A History for Peter*
by Gerald W. Johnson
The Gammage Cup by Carol Kendall
My Side of the Mountain
by Jean Craighead George

1959

WINNER:
The Witch of Blackbird Pond
by Elizabeth George Speare

HONOR BOOKS:
Along Came a Dog
by Meindert DeJong
Chucaro: Wild Pony of the Pampa
by Francis Kalnay
The Family Under the Bridge
by Natalie Savage Carlson
The Perilous Road by William O. Steele

1958

WINNER:
Rifles for Watie by Harold Keith

HONOR BOOKS:
Gone-Away Lake by Elizabeth Enright
The Great Wheel by Robert Lawson
The Horsecatcher by Mari Sandoz
Tom Paine, Freedom's Apostle
by Leo Gurko

1957

WINNER:
Miracles on Maple Hill
by Virginia Sorenson

HONOR BOOKS:
Black Fox of Lorne
by Marguerite de Angeli
The Corn Grows Ripe
by Dorothy Rhoads
The House of Sixty Fathers
by Meindert DeJong

Mr. Justice Holmes
by Clara Ingram Judson

Old Yeller by Fred Gipson

1956

WINNER:
Carry On, Mr. Bowditch
by Jean Lee Latham

HONOR BOOKS:
The Golden Name Day
by Jennie Lindquist

Men, Microscopes, and Living Things
by Katherine Shippen

The Secret River
by Marjorie Kinnan Rawlings

1955

WINNER:
The Wheel on the School
by Meindert DeJong

HONOR BOOKS:
Banner in the Sky by James Ullman

Courage of Sarah Noble
by Alice Dalgliesh

1954

WINNER:
. . . And Now Miguel
by Joseph Krumgold

HONOR BOOKS:
All Alone by Claire Huchet Bishop

Hurry Home, Candy
by Meindert DeJong

Magic Maize by Mary and Conrad Buff

Shadrach by Meindert DeJong

Theodore Roosevelt, Fighting Patriot
by Clara Ingram Judson

1953

WINNER:
Secret of the Andes
by Ann Nolan Clark

HONOR BOOKS:
The Bears on Hemlock Mountain
by Alice Dalgliesh

Birthdays of Freedom, Vol. 1
by Genevieve Foster

Charlotte's Web by E.B. White

Moccasin Trail by Eloise McGraw

Red Sails to Capri by Ann Weil

1952

WINNER:
Ginger Pye by Eleanor Estes

HONOR BOOKS:
Americans Before Columbus
by Elizabeth Baity

The Apple and the Arrow
by Mary and Conrad Buff

The Defender by Nicholas Kalashnikoff

The Light at Tern Rock by Julia Sauer

Minn of the Mississippi
by Holling C. Holling

1951

WINNER:
Amos Fortune, Free Man
by Elizabeth Yates

HONOR BOOKS:
*Abraham Lincoln, Friend
of the People*
by Clara Ingram Judson

Better Known as Johnny Appleseed
by Mabel Leigh Hunt

Gandhi, Fighter without a Sword
by Jeanette Eaton

The Story of Appleby Capple
by Anne Parrish

1950

WINNER:
The Door in the Wall
by Marguerite de Angeli

HONOR BOOKS:
The Blue Cat of Castle Town
by Catherine Coblentz

George Washington
by Genevieve Foster

Kildee House
by Rutherford Montgomery

Song of the Pines: A Story of
Norwegian Lumbering in Wisconsin
by Walter and Marion Havighurst

Tree of Freedom by Rebecca Caudill

1949

WINNER:
King of the Wind by Marguerite Henry

HONOR BOOKS:
Daughter of the Mountain
by Louise Rankin

My Father's Dragon by Ruth S. Gannett

Seabird by Holling C. Holling

Story of the Negro by Arna Bontemps

1948

WINNER:
The Twenty-One Balloons
by William Pène du Bois

HONOR BOOKS:
*The Cow-Tail Switch, and
Other West African Stories*
by Harold Courlander

Li Lun, Lad of Courage
by Carolyn Treffinger

Misty of Chincoteague
by Marguertie Henry

Pancakes-Paris
by Claire Huchet Bishop

*The Quaint and Curious Quest
of Johnny Longfoot*
by Catherine Besterman

1947

WINNER:
Miss Hickory by Carolyn Sherwin Bailey

HONOR BOOKS:
The Avion My Uncle Flew
by Cyrus Fisher

Big Tree by Mary and Conrad Buff

The Heavenly Tenants
by William Maxwell

The Hidden Treasure of Glaston
by Eleanor Jewett

Wonderful Year by Nancy Barnes

1946

WINNER:
Strawberry Girl by Lois Lenski

HONOR BOOKS:
Bhimsa, the Dancing Bear
by Christine Weston

Justin Morgan Had a Horse
by Marguerite Henry

The Moved-Outers
by Florence Crannell Means

New Found World
by Katherine Shippen

1945

WINNER:
Rabbit Hill by Robert Lawson

HONOR BOOKS:
Abraham Lincoln's World
by Genevieve Foster

The Hundred Dresses
by Eleanor Estes

*Lone Journey: The Life of
Roger Williams*
by Jeanette Eaton

The Silver Pencil by Alice Dalgliesh

1944

WINNER:
Johnny Tremain by Esther Forbes

HONOR BOOKS:
Fog Magic by Julia Sauer

Mountain Born by Elizabeth Yates

Rufus M. by Eleanor Estes

These Happy Golden Years
by Laura Ingalls Wilder

1943

WINNER:
Adam of the Road
by Elizabeth Janet Gray

HONOR BOOKS:
Have You Seen Tom Thumb?
by Mabel Leigh Hunt

The Middle Moffat by Eleanor Estes

1942

WINNER:
The Matchlock Gun
by Walter D. Edmonds

HONOR BOOKS:
Down Ryton Water by Eva Roe Gaggin

George Washington's World
by Genevieve Foster

*Indian Captive: The Story
of Mary Jemison*
by Lois Lenski

Little Town on the Prairie
by Laura Ingalls Wilder

1941

WINNER:
Call It Courage by Armstrong Sperry

HONOR BOOKS:
Blue Willow by Doris Gates

The Long Winter
by Laura Ingalls Wilder

Nansen by Anna Gertrude Hall

Young Mac of Fort Vancouver
by Mary Jane Carr

1940

WINNER:
Daniel Boone by James Daugherty

HONOR BOOKS:
Boy with a Pack by Stephen W. Meader

By the Shores of Silver Lake
by Laura Ingalls Wilder

*Runner of the Mountain Tops:
The Life of Louis Agassiz*
by Mabel Robinson

The Singing Tree by Kate Seredy

1939

WINNER:
Thimble Summer by Elizabeth Enright

HONOR BOOKS:
Hello the Boat! by Phyllis Crawford

*Leader by Destiny: George
Washington, Man and Patriot*
by Jeanette Eaton

Mr. Popper's Penguins
by Richard and Florence Atwater

Nino by Valenti Angelo

Penn by Elizabeth Janet Gray

1938

WINNER:
The White Stag by Kate Seredy

HONOR BOOKS:
Bright Island by Mabel Robinson

On the Banks of Plum Creek
by Laura Ingalls Wilder

Pecos Bill by James Cloyd Bowman

1937

WINNER:
Roller Skates by Ruth Sawyer

HONOR BOOKS:
Audubon by Constance Rourke

The Codfish Musket by Agnes Hewes

The Golden Basket
by Ludwig Bemelmans

Phoebe Fairchild: Her Book
by Lois Lenski

Whistler's Van by Idwal Jones

Winterbound by Margery Bianco

1936

WINNER:
Caddie Woodlawn by Carol Ryrie Brink

HONOR BOOKS:
*All Sail Set: A Romance of
the Flying Cloud*
by Armstrong Sperry

The Good Master by Kate Seredy

Honk, the Moose by Phil Stong

Young Walter Scott
by Elizabeth Janet Gray

1935

WINNER:
Dobry by Monica Shannon

HONOR BOOKS:
Davy Crockett by Constance Rourke

*Days on Skates: The Story
of a Dutch Picnic*
by Hilda Von Stockum

Pageant of Chinese History
by Elizabeth Seeger

1934

WINNER:
*Invincible Louisa: The Story
of the Author of* Little Women
by Cornelia Meigs

HONOR BOOKS:
ABC Bunny by Wanda Gág

Apprentice of Florence by Ann Kyle

*Big Tree of Bunlahy: Stories
of My Own Countryside*
by Padraic Colum

The Forgotten Daughter
by Caroline Snedeker

Glory of the Seas by Agnes Hewes

New Land by Sarah Schmidt

Swords of Steel
by Elsie Singmaster

Winged Girl of Knossos
by Erik Berry

1933

WINNER:
Young Fu of the Upper Yangtze
by Elizabeth Lewis

HONOR BOOKS:
*Children of the Soil: A
Story of Scandinavia*
by Nora Burglon

*The Railroad to Freedom:
A Story of the Civil War*
by Hildegarde Swift

Swift Rivers by Cornelia Meigs

1932

WINNER:
Waterless Mountain
by Laura Adams Armer

HONOR BOOKS:
Boy of the South Seas
by Eunice Tietjens

Calico Bush by Rachel Field

The Fairy Circus by Dorothy P. Lathrop

Jane's Island by Marjorie Allee

Out of the Flame by Eloise Lownsbery

*Truce of the Wolf and Other
Tales of Old Italy*
by Mary Gould Davis

1931

WINNER:
The Cat Who Went to Heaven
by Elizabeth Coatsworth

HONOR BOOKS:
*The Dark Star of Itza: The
Story of a Pagan Princess*
by Alida Malkus

Floating Island by Anne Parrish

*Garram the Hunter: A Boy
of the Hill Tribes*
by Herbert Best

Meggy Macintosh
by Elizabeth Janet Gray

Mountains Are Free
by Julia Davis Adams

Ood-Le-Uk the Wanderer
by Alice Lide and Margaret Johansen

Queer Person by Ralph Hubbard

Spice and the Devil's Cake
by Agnes Hewes

1930

WINNER:
Hitty, Her First Hundred Years
by Rachel Field

HONOR BOOKS:
*A Daughter of the Seine: The
Life of Madam Roland*
by Jeanette Eaton

Jumping-Off Place
by Marian Hurd McNeely

Little Blacknose by Hildegarde Swift

Pran of Albania by Elizabeth Miller

*The Tangle-Coated Horse
and Other Tales*
by Ella Young

Vaino by Julia Davis Adams

1929

WINNER:
The Trumpeter of Krakow
by Eric P. Kelly

HONOR BOOKS:
The Boy Who Was by Grace Hallock
Clearing Weather by Cornelia Meigs
Millions of Cats by Wanda Gág
Pigtail of Ah Lee Ben Loo
by John Bennett
Runaway Papoose by Grace Moon
Tod of the Fens by Elinor Whitney

1928

WINNER:
Gay Neck, the Story of a Pigeon
by Dhan Gopal Mukerji

HONOR BOOKS:
Downright Dencey
by Caroline Snedeker
The Wonder Smith and His Son
by Ella Young

1927

WINNER:
Smoky, the Cowhorse by Will James

1926

WINNER:
Shen of the Sea
by Arthur Bowie Chrisman

HONOR BOOK:
*The Voyagers: Being Legends and
Romances of Atlantic Discovery*
by Padraic Colum

1925

WINNER:
Tales from Silver Lands
by Charles Finger

HONOR BOOKS:
The Dream Coach by Anne Parrish
*Nicholas: A Manhattan
Christmas Story*
by Annie Carroll Moore

1924

WINNER:
The Dark Frigate
by Charles Boardman Hawes

1923

WINNER:
The Voyages of Doctor Doolittle
by Hugh Lofting

1922

WINNER:
The Story of Mankind
by Hendrik Willem van Loon

HONOR BOOKS:
Cedric the Forester
by Bernard Marshall
*The Golden Fleece and the Heroes
Who Lived Before Achilles*
by Padraic Colum
The Great Quest
by Charles Boardman Hawes
*The Old Tobacco Shop: A True
Account of What Befell a Little
Boy in Search of Adventure*
by William Bowen
The Windy Hill by Cornelia Meigs